PHILIP PULLMAN

THE GOLDEN COMPASS
THE GRAPHIC NOVEL

VOLUME TWO

Adapted by Stéphane Melchior, art by Clément Oubrerie
Coloring by Clément Oubrerie with Philippe Bruno
Translated by Annie Eaton

ALFRED A. KNOPF  NEW YORK

THIS IS A BORZOI BOOK PUBLISHED BY ALFRED A. KNOPF

Visit us on the Web! randomhousekids.com

Educators and librarians, for a variety of teaching tools, visit us at RHTeachersLibrarians.com

Library of Congress Cataloging-in-Publication Data is available upon request.
ISBN 978-0-553-53512-9 (hc) — ISBN 978-0-553-53514-3 (lib. bdg.)
ISBN 978-0-553-53513-6 (pbk.) — ISBN 978-0-553-53515-0 (ebook)

MANUFACTURED IN CHINA
September 2016
10 9 8 7 6 5 4 3 2 1

First U.S. Edition

Rescued by the gyptians, Lyra is traveling north to find Lord Asriel and save her friend Roger. . . .

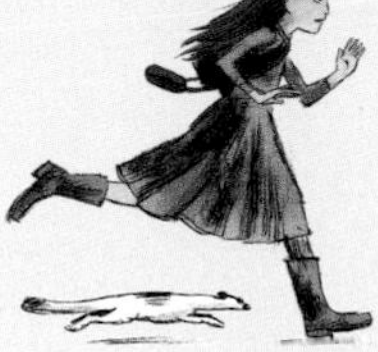

LYRA thought she was an orphan but recently learned that Mrs. Coulter and Lord Asriel are her true parents.

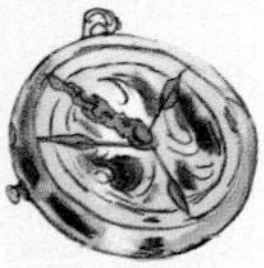

THE ALETHIOMETER, a rare instrument that allows the reader to find out the truth, was entrusted to Lyra by the Master of Jordan College.

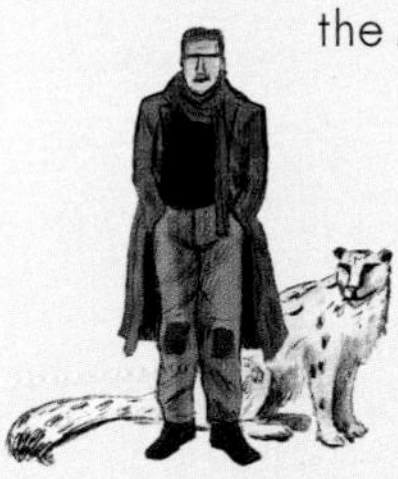

LORD ASRIEL, who is investigating the mysterious substance known as Dust, is being held prisoner by armored bears in remote Svalbard.

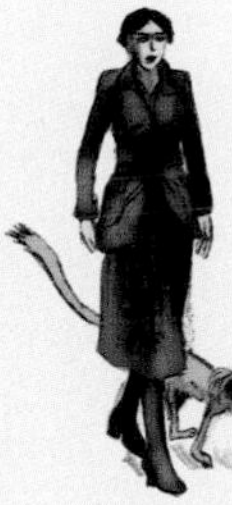

MRS. COULTER, head of the General Oblation Board, is probably behind the child-snatching Gobblers.

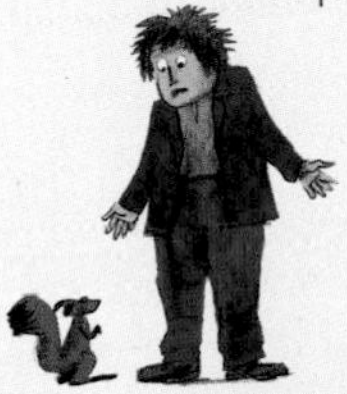

ROGER, Lyra's best friend, has been kidnapped by the Gobblers.

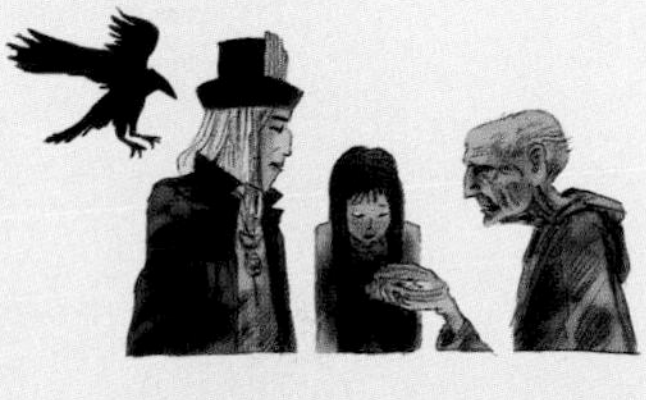

JOHN FAA, king of the gyptians, is leading an expedition north to rescue the children taken by the Gobblers. FARDER CORAM, the oldest of the gyptians, revealed to Lyra the identity of her parents. He once saved the life of a witch—whose help will prove invaluable.

For my father, Claude
—S.M.

Friendly wishes to F'murr, also to J.J. and Gégé, who, each in their own way,
have given me a love of wide snowy spaces
—C.O.

The word "dœmon," which appears throughout this book, is pronounced like "demon."

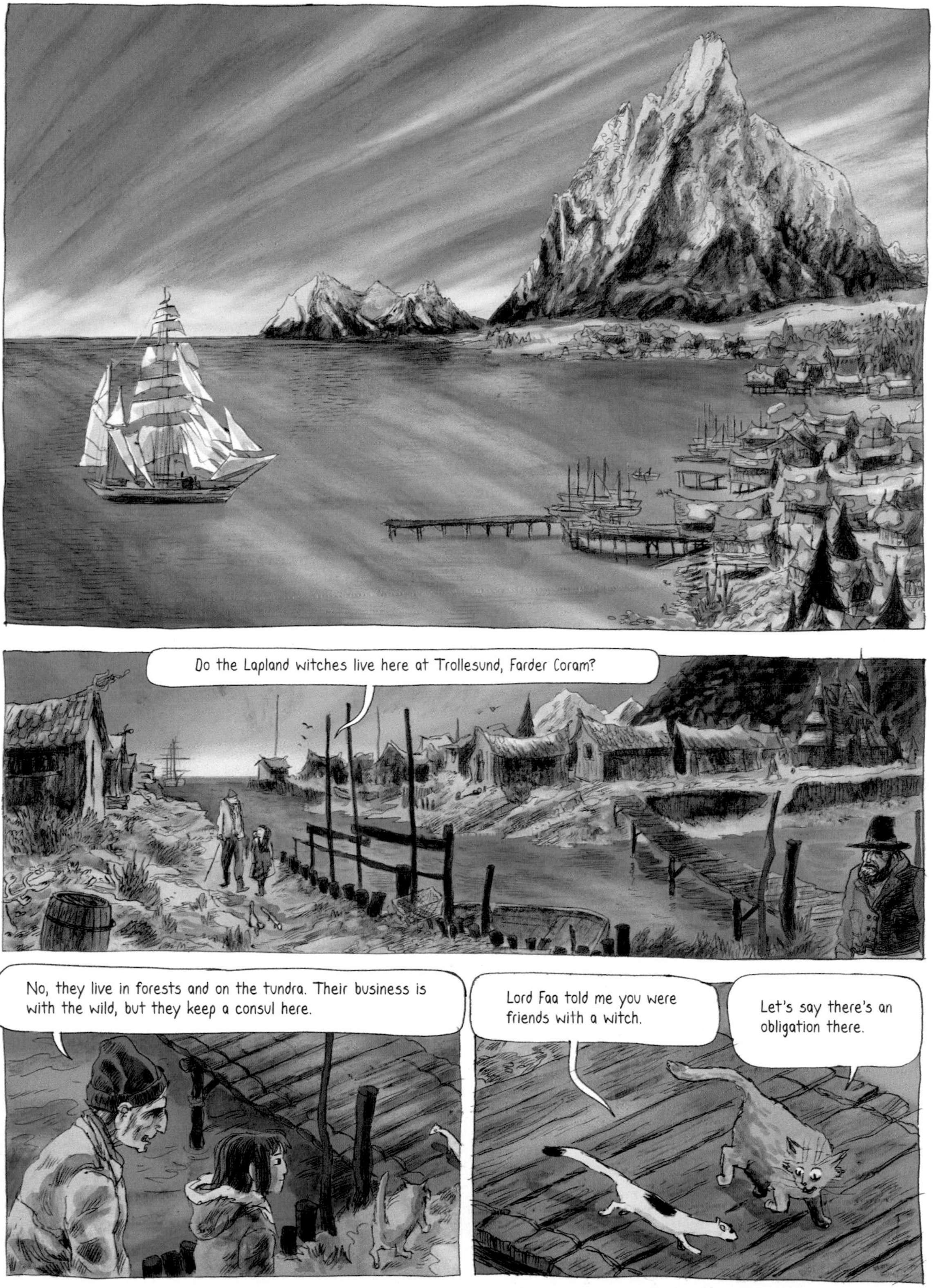
Do the Lapland witches live here at Trollesund, Farder Coram?
No, they live in forests and on the tundra. Their business is with the wild, but they keep a consul here.
Lord Faa told me you were friends with a witch.
Let's say there's an obligation there.

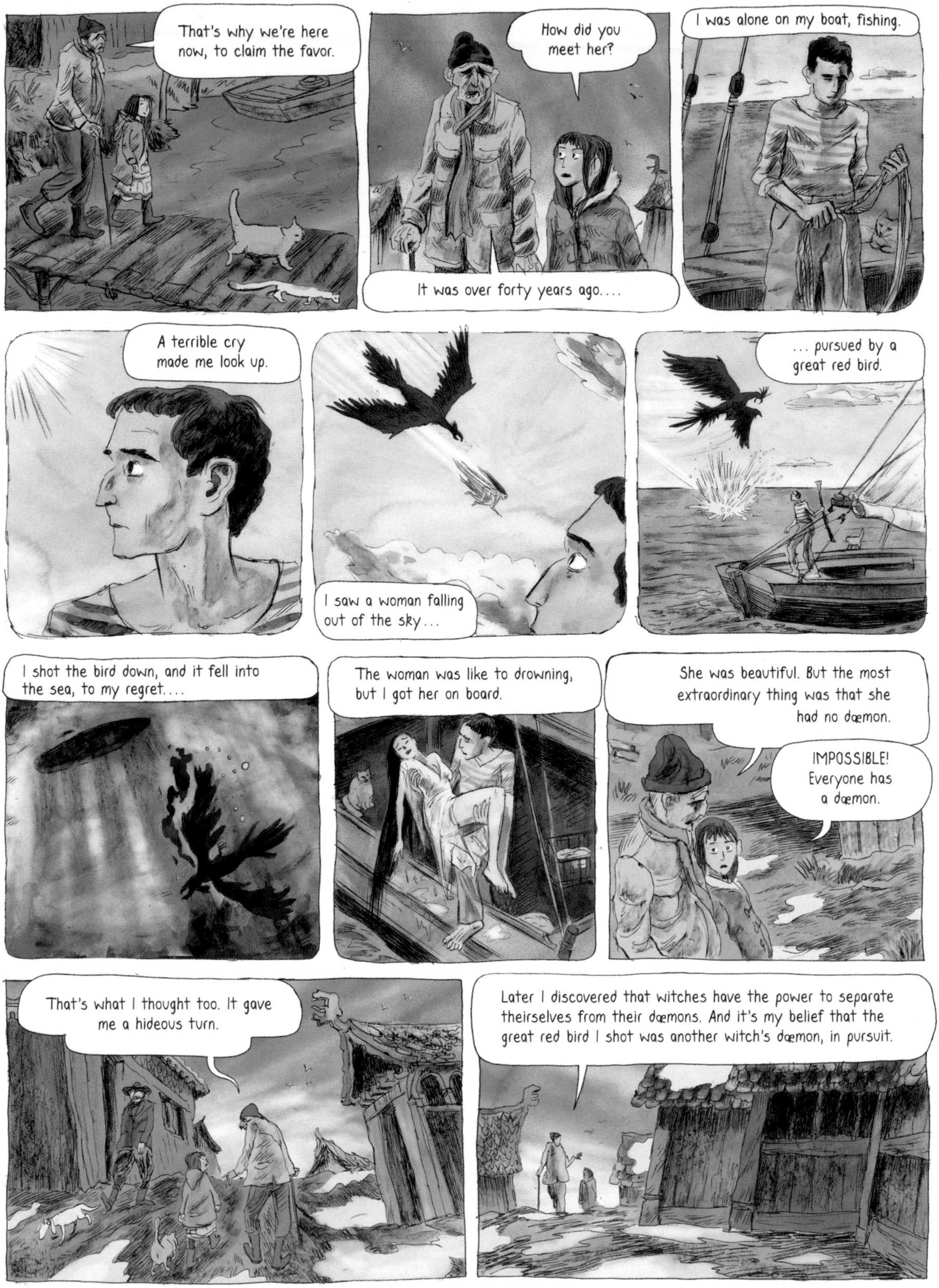

That's why we're here now, to claim the favor.
How did you meet her?
It was over forty years ago....
I was alone on my boat, fishing.
A terrible cry made me look up.
I saw a woman falling out of the sky...
... pursued by a great red bird.
I shot the bird down, and it fell into the sea, to my regret....
The woman was like to drowning, but I got her on board.
She was beautiful. But the most extraordinary thing was that she had no dæmon.
IMPOSSIBLE! Everyone has a dæmon.
That's what I thought too. It gave me a hideous turn.
Later I discovered that witches have the power to separate theirselves from their dæmons. And it's my belief that the great red bird I shot was another witch's dæmon, in pursuit.

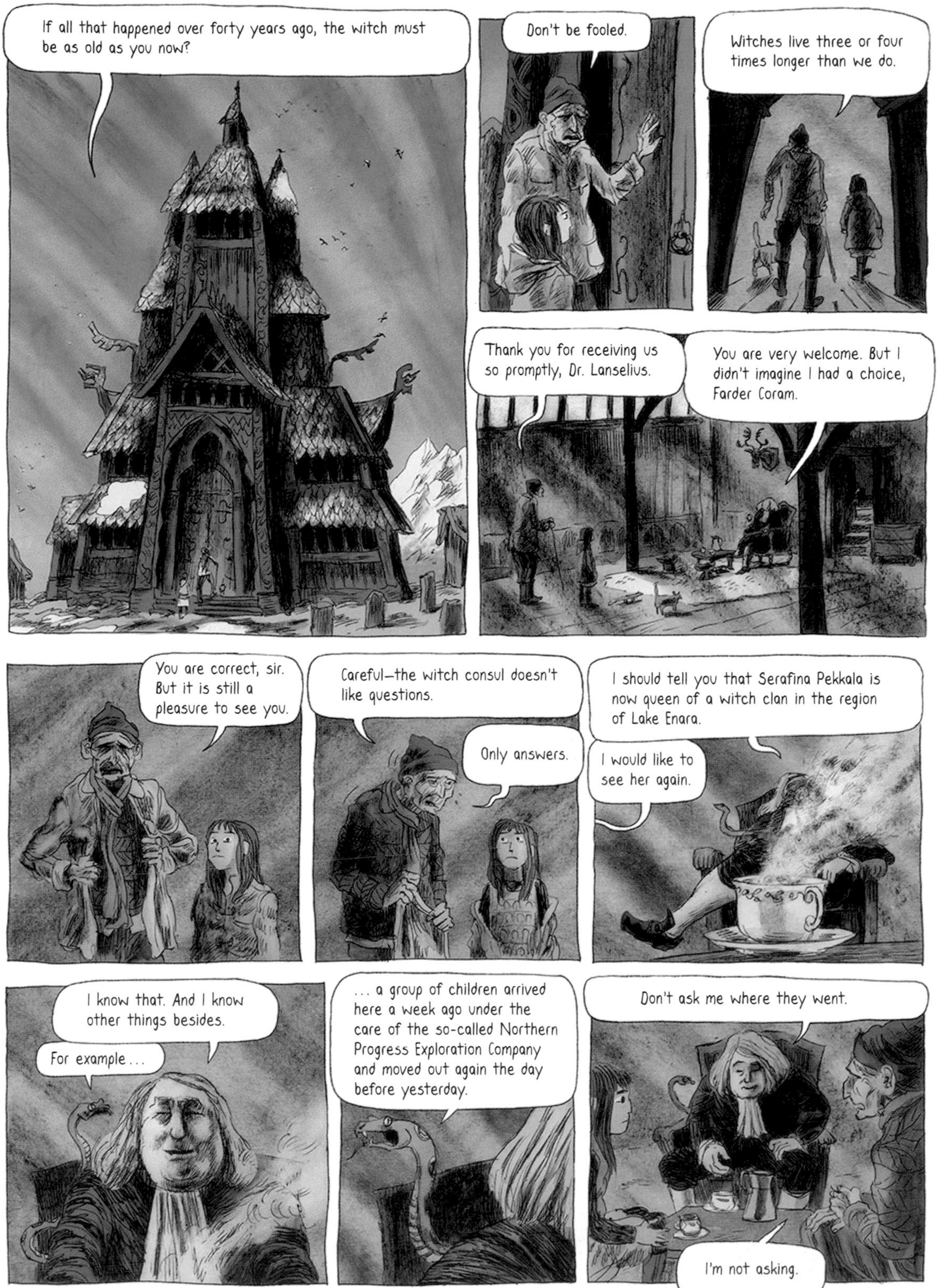
If all that happened over forty years ago, the witch must be as old as you now?
Don't be fooled.
Witches live three or four times longer than we do.
Thank you for receiving us so promptly, Dr. Lanselius.
You are very welcome. But I didn't imagine I had a choice, Farder Coram.
You are correct, sir. But it is still a pleasure to see you.
Careful—the witch consul doesn't like questions.
Only answers.
I should tell you that Serafina Pekkala is now queen of a witch clan in the region of Lake Enara.
I would like to see her again.
I know that. And I know other things besides.
For example . . .
. . . a group of children arrived here a week ago under the care of the so-called Northern Progress Exploration Company and moved out again the day before yesterday.
Don't ask me where they went.
I'm not asking.

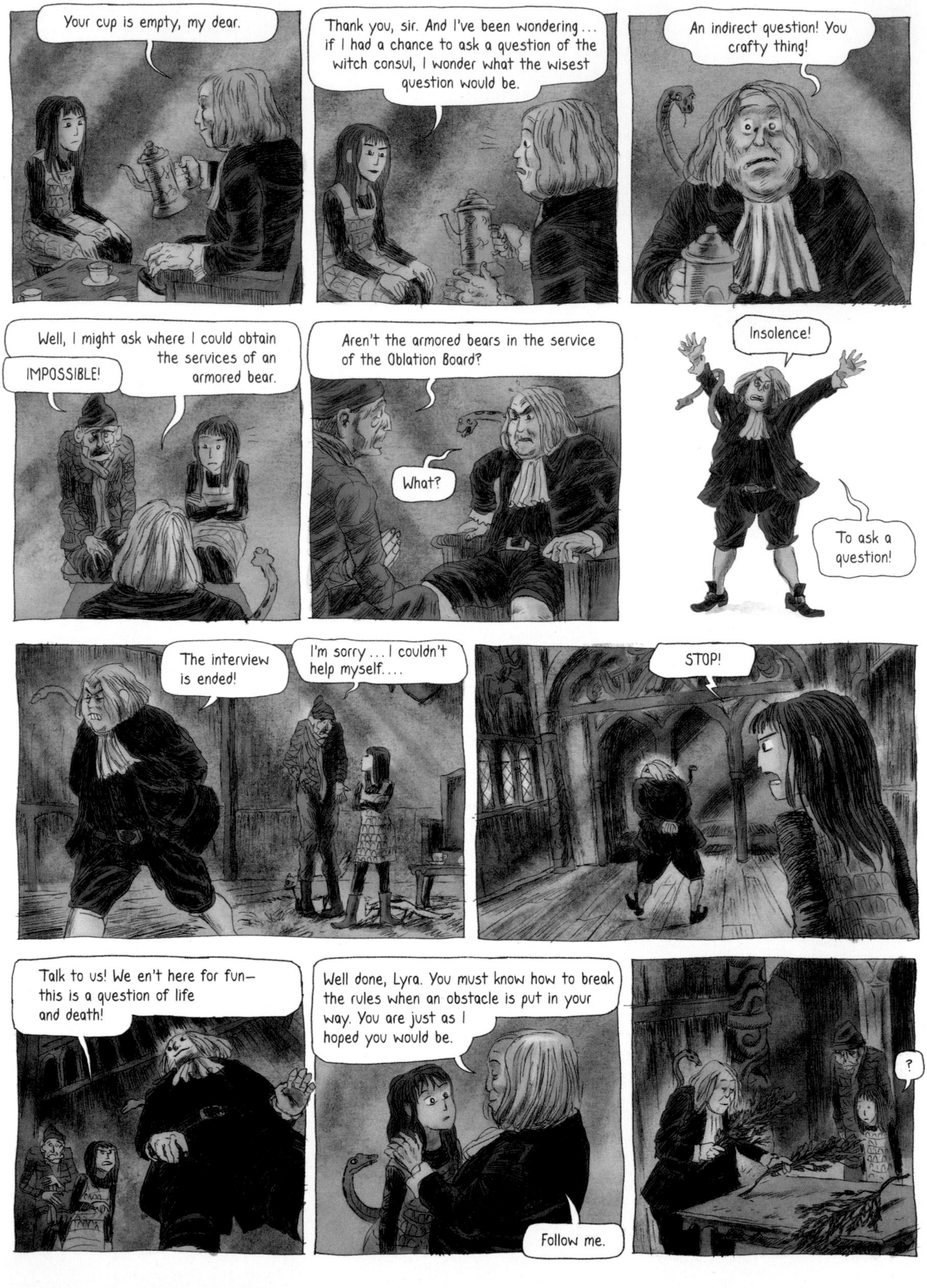

Your cup is empty, my dear.
Thank you, sir. And I've been wondering... if I had a chance to ask a question of the witch consul, I wonder what the wisest question would be.
An indirect question! You crafty thing!
Well, I might ask where I could obtain the services of an armored bear.
IMPOSSIBLE!
Aren't the armored bears in the service of the Oblation Board?
What?
Insolence!
To ask a question!
The interview is ended!
I'm sorry... I couldn't help myself....
STOP!
Talk to us! We en't here for fun—this is a question of life and death!
Well done, Lyra. You must know how to break the rules when an obstacle is put in your way. You are just as I hoped you would be.
Follow me.
?

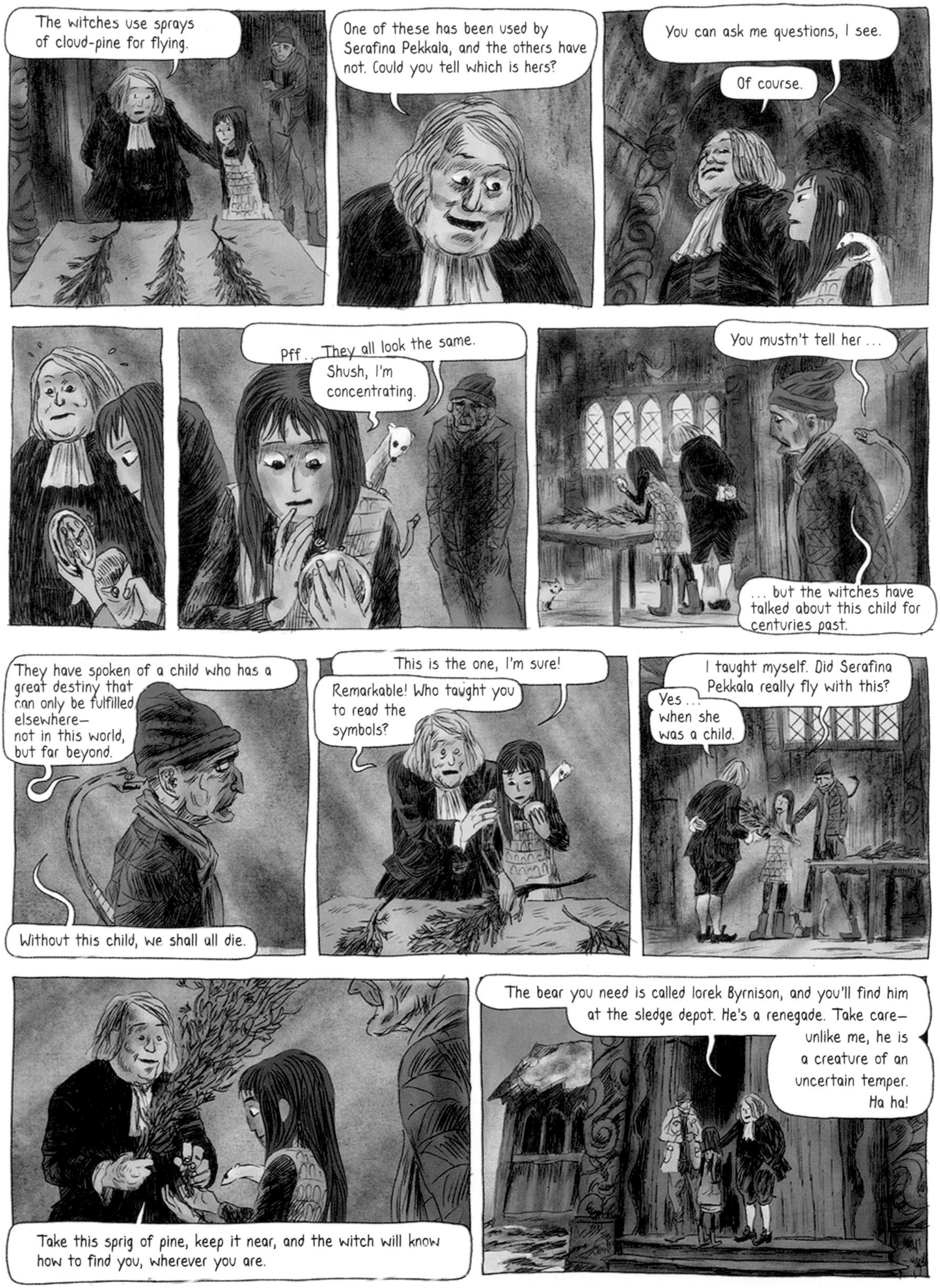
The witches use sprays of cloud-pine for flying.
One of these has been used by Serafina Pekkala, and the others have not. Could you tell which is hers?
You can ask me questions, I see.
Of course.
Pff... They all look the same.
Shush, I'm concentrating.
You mustn't tell her...
... but the witches have talked about this child for centuries past.
They have spoken of a child who has a great destiny that can only be fulfilled elsewhere— not in this world, but far beyond.
Without this child, we shall all die.
This is the one, I'm sure!
Remarkable! Who taught you to read the symbols?
I taught myself. Did Serafina Pekkala really fly with this?
Yes... when she was a child.
Take this sprig of pine, keep it near, and the witch will know how to find you, wherever you are.
The bear you need is called Iorek Byrnison, and you'll find him at the sledge depot. He's a renegade. Take care— unlike me, he is a creature of an uncertain temper. Ha ha!

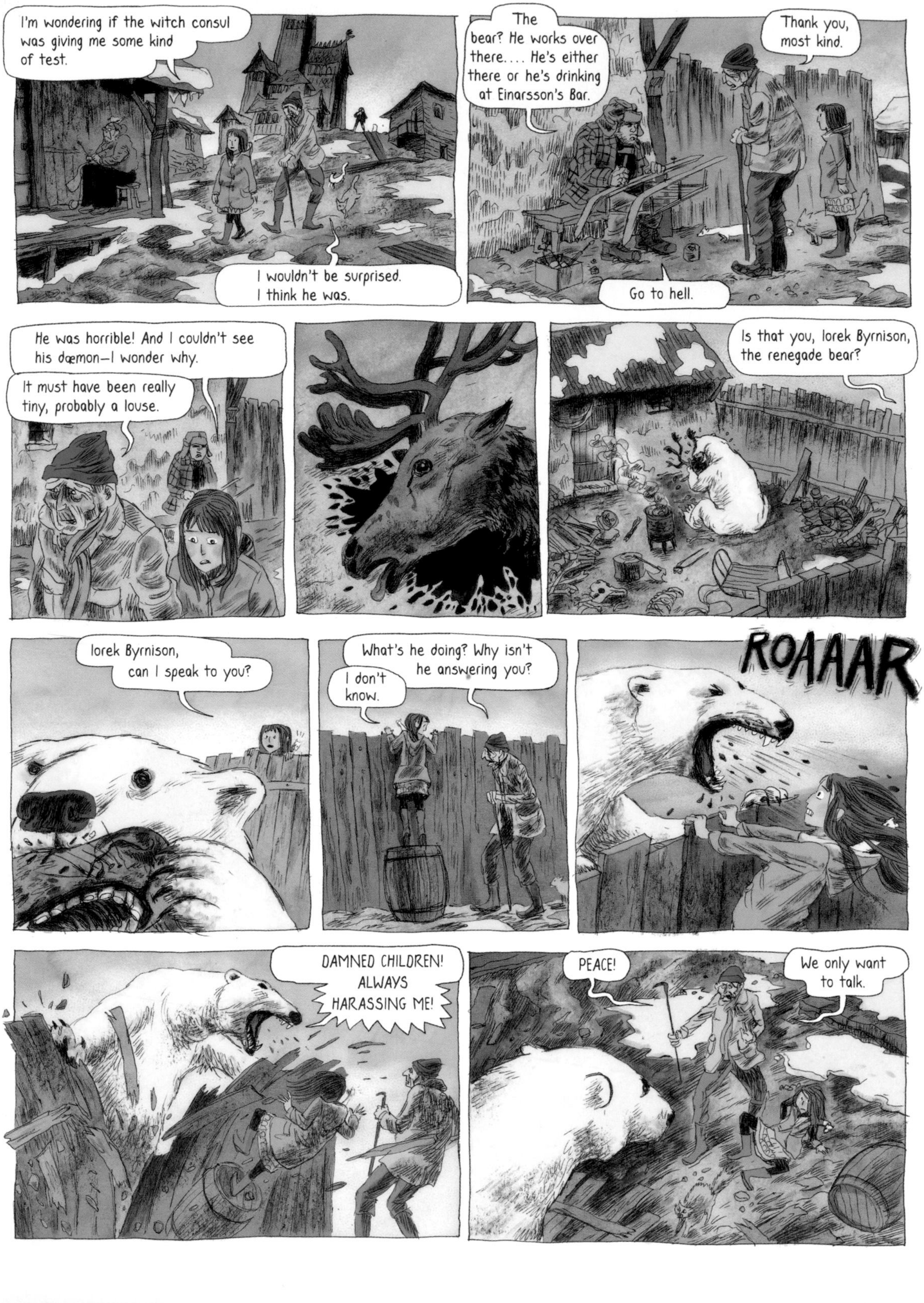

I'm wondering if the witch consul was giving me some kind of test.
I wouldn't be surprised. I think he was.
The bear? He works over there.... He's either there or he's drinking at Einarsson's Bar.
Thank you, most kind.
Go to hell.
He was horrible! And I couldn't see his dæmon—I wonder why.
It must have been really tiny, probably a louse.
Is that you, Iorek Byrnison, the renegade bear?
Iorek Byrnison, can I speak to you?
What's he doing? Why isn't he answering you?
I don't know.
ROAAAR
DAMNED CHILDREN! ALWAYS HARASSING ME!
PEACE!
We only want to talk.

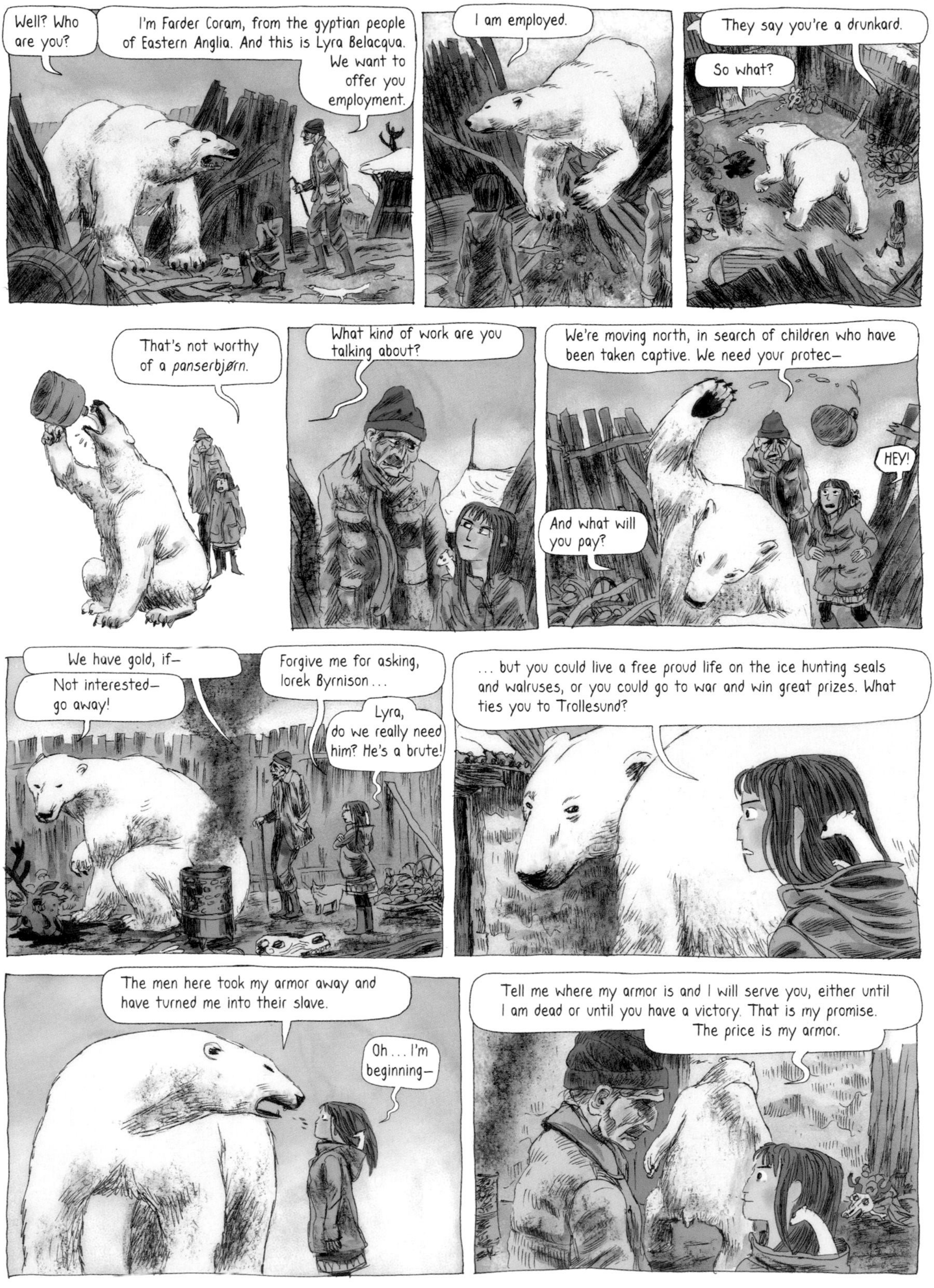

Well? Who are you?
I'm Farder Coram, from the gyptian people of Eastern Anglia. And this is Lyra Belacqua. We want to offer you employment.
I am employed.
They say you're a drunkard.
So what?
That's not worthy of a *panserbjørn*.
What kind of work are you talking about?
We're moving north, in search of children who have been taken captive. We need your protec—
HEY!
And what will you pay?
We have gold, if—
Not interested— go away!
Forgive me for asking, Iorek Byrnison...
Lyra, do we really need him? He's a brute!
... but you could live a free proud life on the ice hunting seals and walruses, or you could go to war and win great prizes. What ties you to Trollesund?
The men here took my armor away and have turned me into their slave.
Oh... I'm beginning—
Tell me where my armor is and I will serve you, either until I am dead or until you have a victory. That is my promise.
The price is my armor.

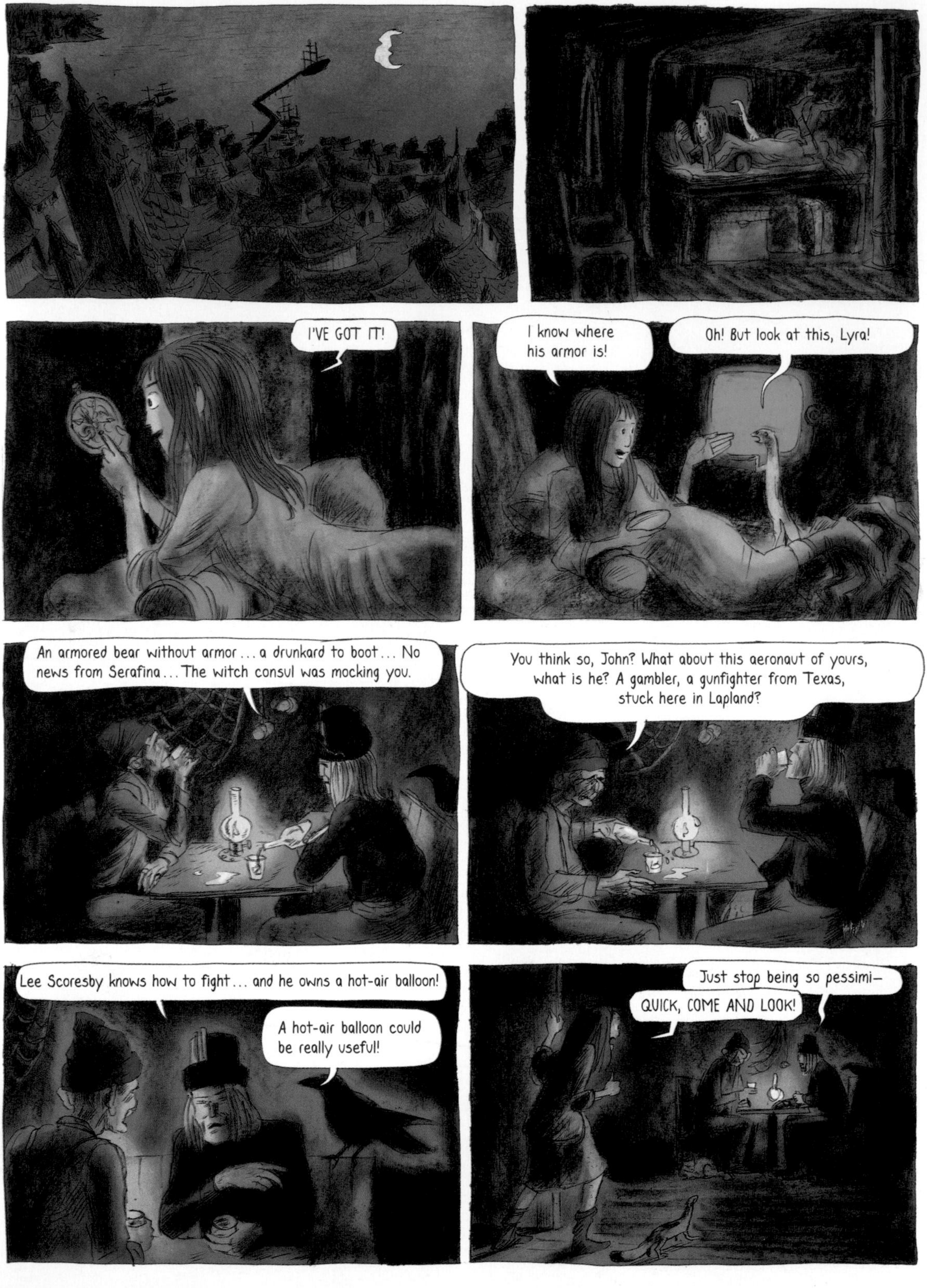
I'VE GOT IT!
I know where his armor is!
Oh! But look at this, Lyra!
An armored bear without armor . . . a drunkard to boot . . . No news from Serafina . . . The witch consul was mocking you.
You think so, John? What about this aeronaut of yours, what is he? A gambler, a gunfighter from Texas, stuck here in Lapland?
Lee Scoresby knows how to fight . . . and he owns a hot-air balloon!
A hot-air balloon could be really useful!
Just stop being so pessimi—
QUICK, COME AND LOOK!

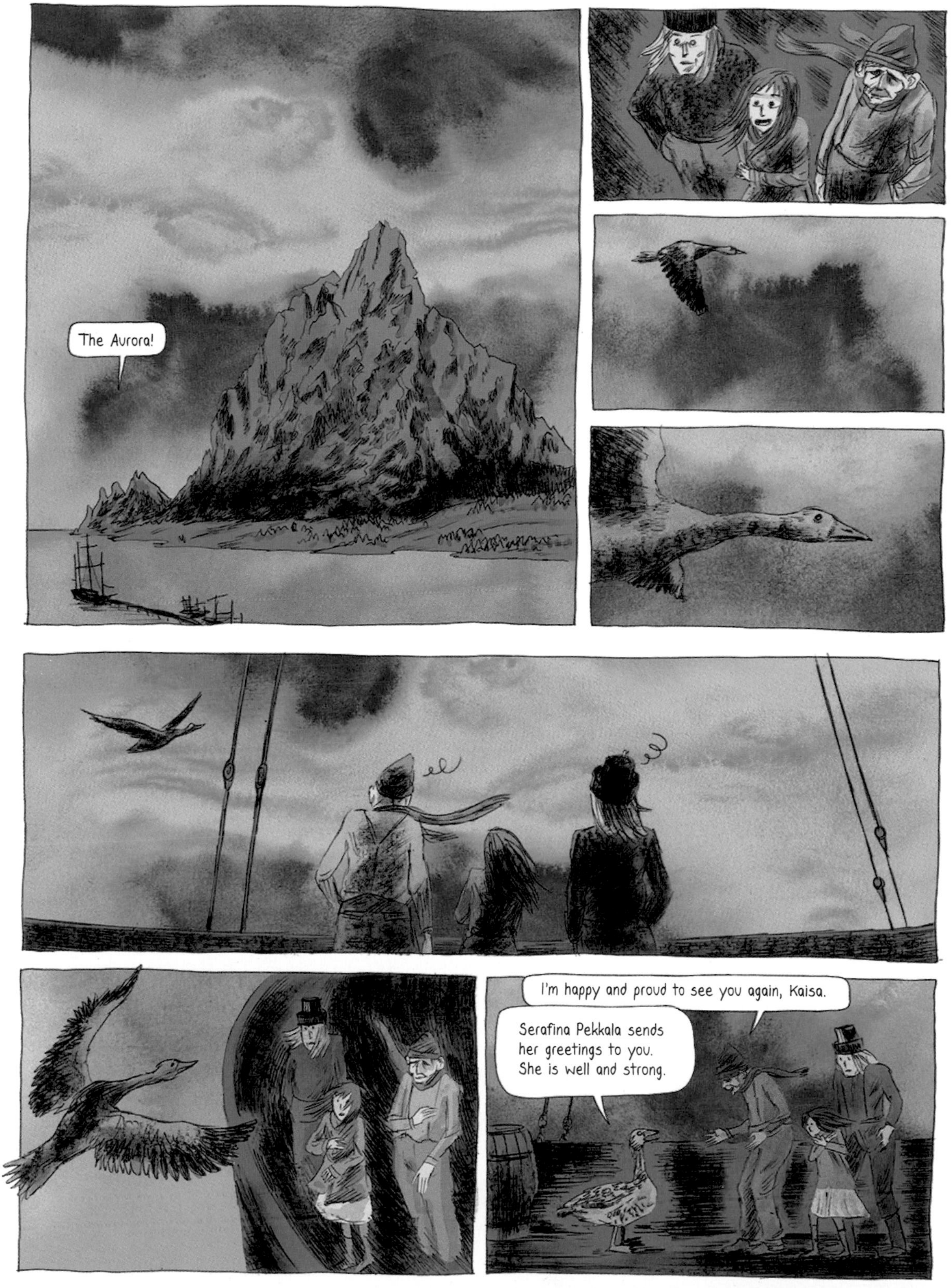
The Aurora!
I'm happy and proud to see you again, Kaisa.
Serafina Pekkala sends her greetings to you. She is well and strong.

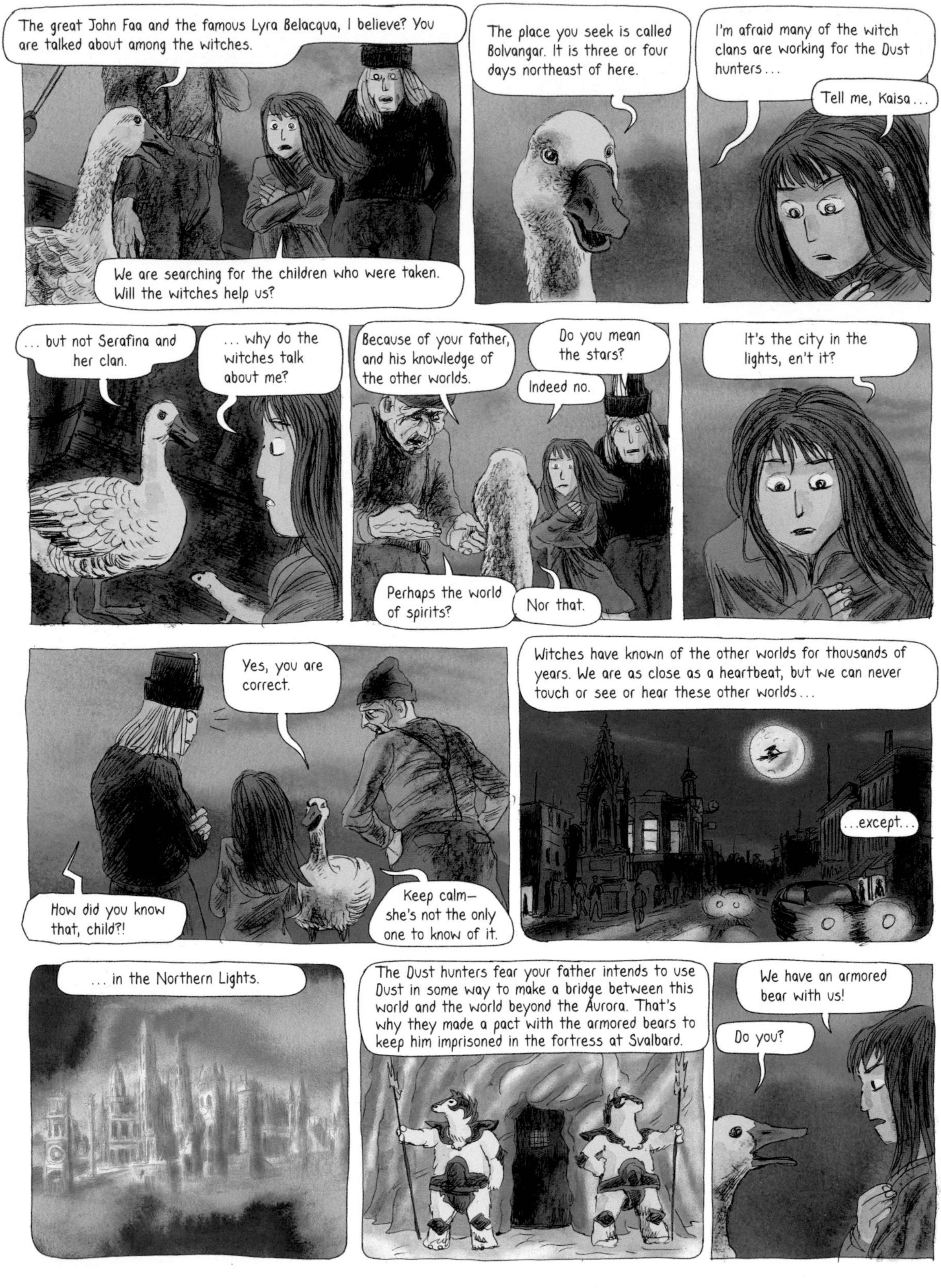
The great John Faa and the famous Lyra Belacqua, I believe? You are talked about among the witches.
We are searching for the children who were taken. Will the witches help us?
The place you seek is called Bolvangar. It is three or four days northeast of here.
I'm afraid many of the witch clans are working for the Dust hunters...
Tell me, Kaisa...
... but not Serafina and her clan.
... why do the witches talk about me?
Because of your father, and his knowledge of the other worlds.
Do you mean the stars?
Indeed no.
Perhaps the world of spirits?
Nor that.
It's the city in the lights, en't it?
Yes, you are correct.
How did you know that, child?!
Keep calm— she's not the only one to know of it.
Witches have known of the other worlds for thousands of years. We are as close as a heartbeat, but we can never touch or see or hear these other worlds...
...except...
... in the Northern Lights.
The Dust hunters fear your father intends to use Dust in some way to make a bridge between this world and the world beyond the Aurora. That's why they made a pact with the armored bears to keep him imprisoned in the fortress at Svalbard.
We have an armored bear with us!
Do you?

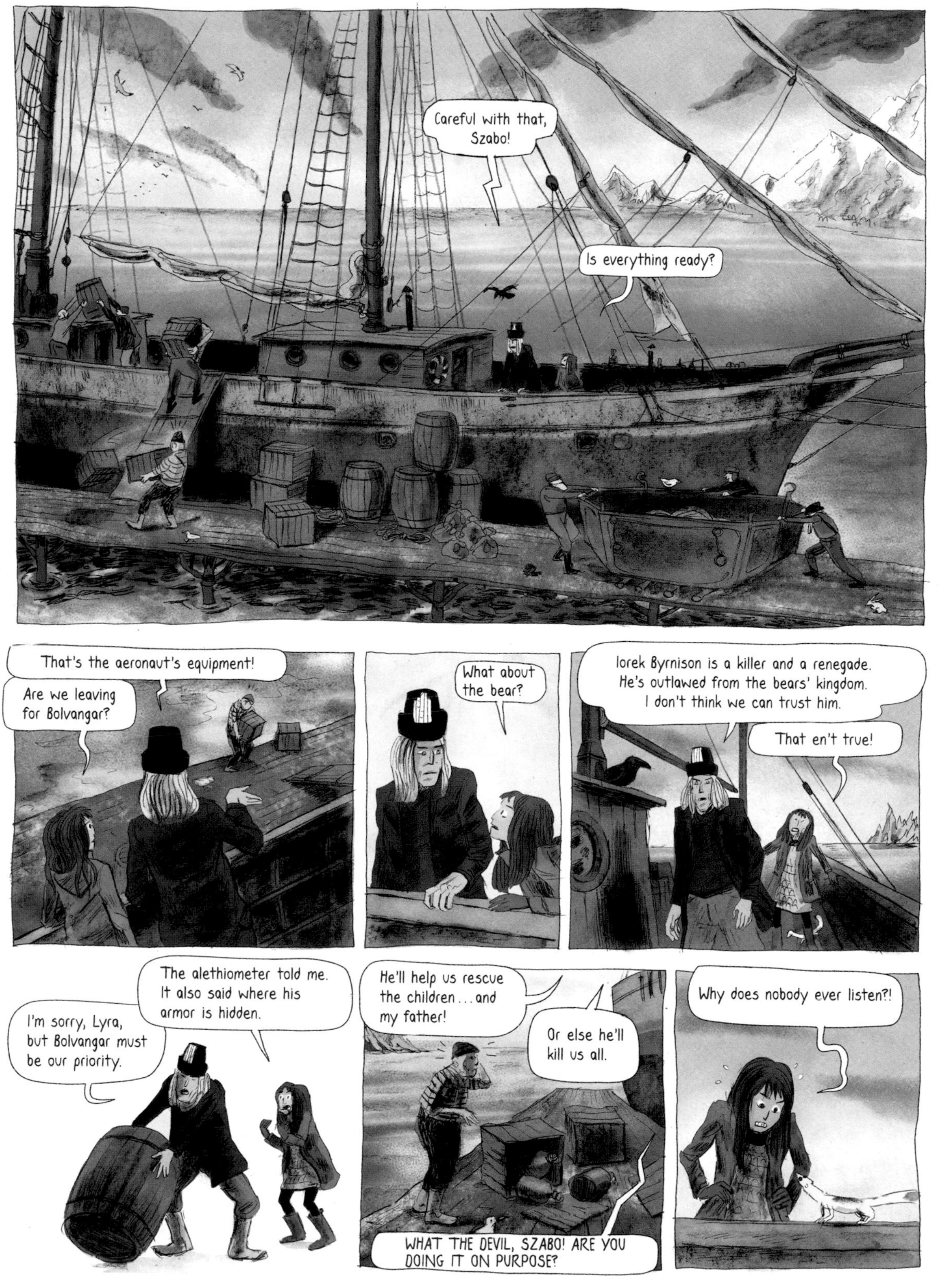
Careful with that, Szabo!
Is everything ready?
That's the aeronaut's equipment!
Are we leaving for Bolvangar?
What about the bear?
Iorek Byrnison is a killer and a renegade. He's outlawed from the bears' kingdom. I don't think we can trust him.
That en't true!
The alethiometer told me. It also said where his armor is hidden.
I'm sorry, Lyra, but Bolvangar must be our priority.
He'll help us rescue the children... and my father!
Or else he'll kill us all.
WHAT THE DEVIL, SZABO! ARE YOU DOING IT ON PURPOSE?
Why does nobody ever listen?!

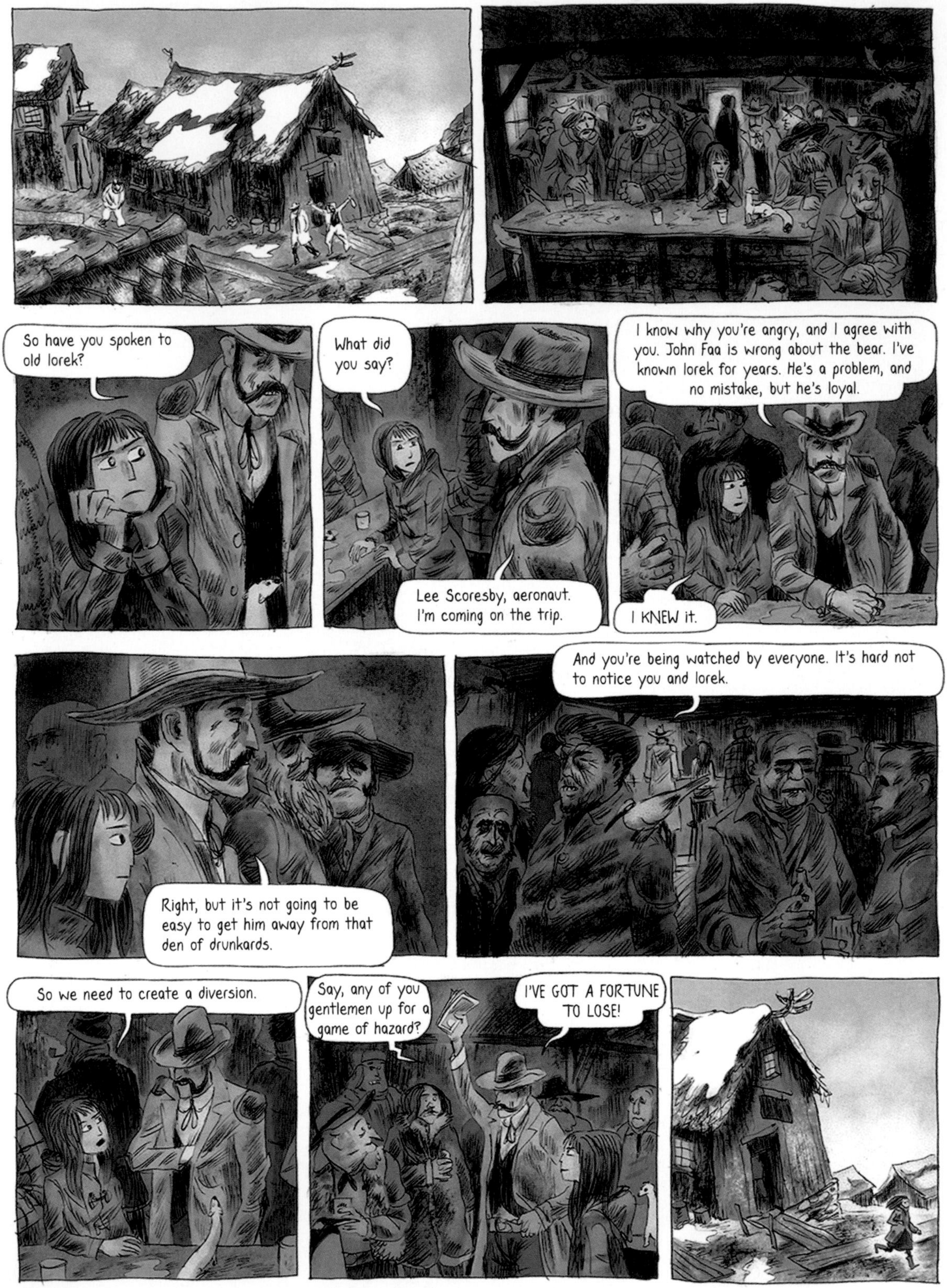
So have you spoken to old lorek?
What did you say?
Lee Scoresby, aeronaut. I'm coming on the trip.
I know why you're angry, and I agree with you. John Faa is wrong about the bear. I've known lorek for years. He's a problem, and no mistake, but he's loyal.
I KNEW it.
Right, but it's not going to be easy to get him away from that den of drunkards.
And you're being watched by everyone. It's hard not to notice you and lorek.
So we need to create a diversion.
Say, any of you gentlemen up for a game of hazard?
I'VE GOT A FORTUNE TO LOSE!

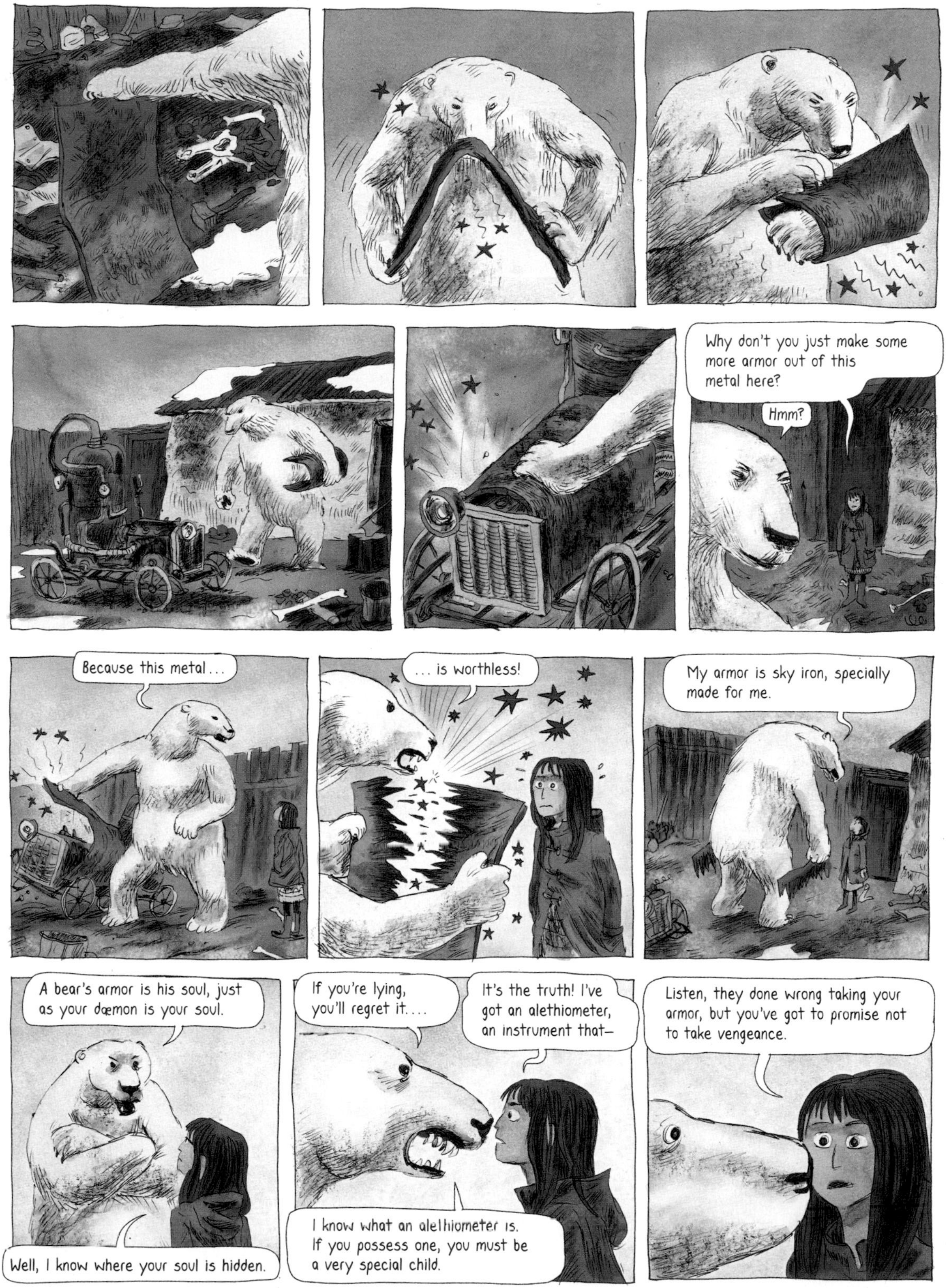

Why don't you just make some more armor out of this metal here?
Hmm?
Because this metal . . .
. . . is worthless!
My armor is sky iron, specially made for me.
A bear's armor is his soul, just as your dæmon is your soul.
Well, I know where your soul is hidden.
If you're lying, you'll regret it. . . .
It's the truth! I've got an alethiometer, an instrument that—
I know what an alethiometer is. If you possess one, you must be a very special child.
Listen, they done wrong taking your armor, but you've got to promise not to take vengeance.

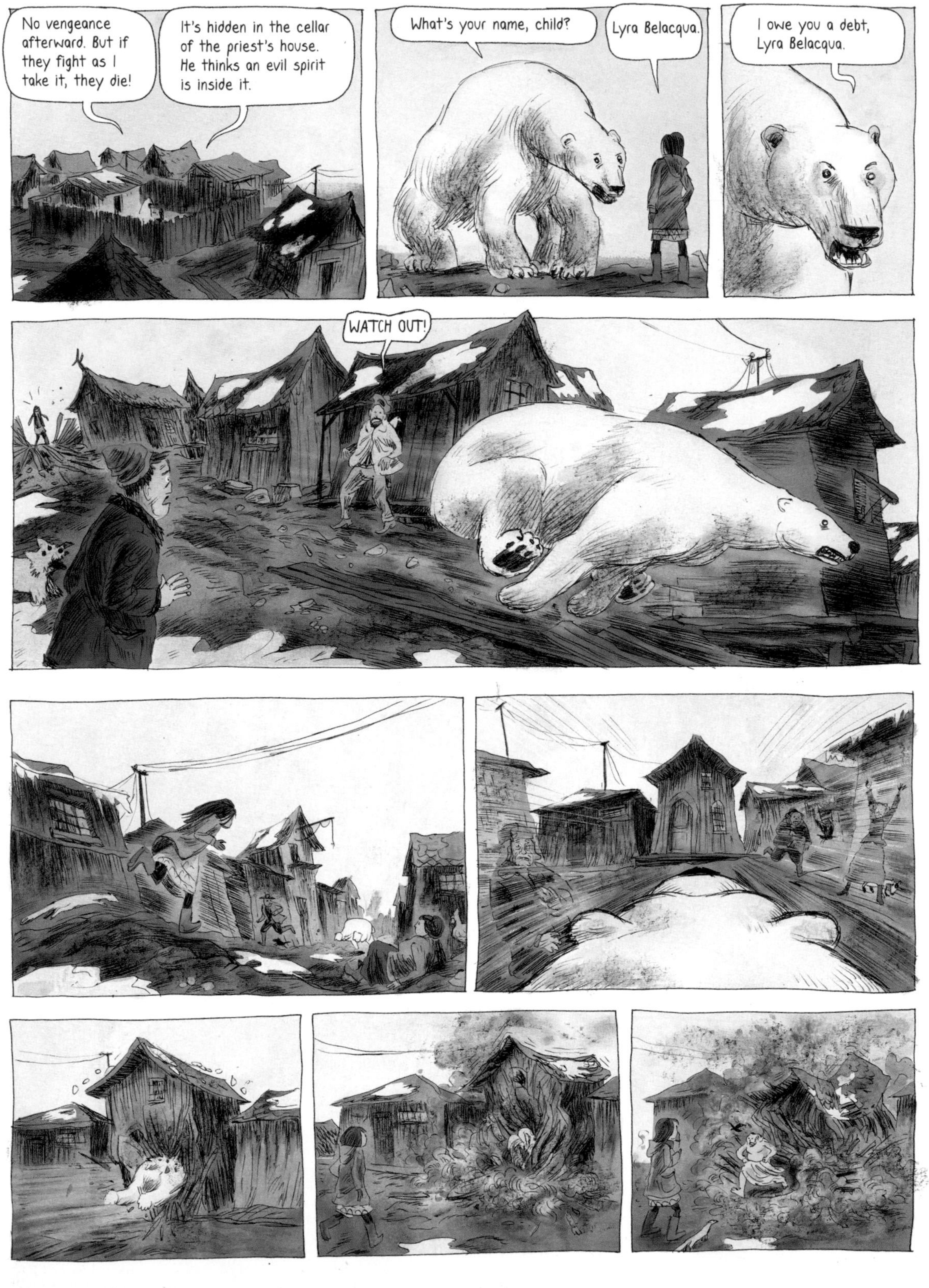
No vengeance afterward. But if they fight as I take it, they die!
It's hidden in the cellar of the priest's house. He thinks an evil spirit is inside it.
What's your name, child?
Lyra Belacqua.
I owe you a debt, Lyra Belacqua.
WATCH OUT!

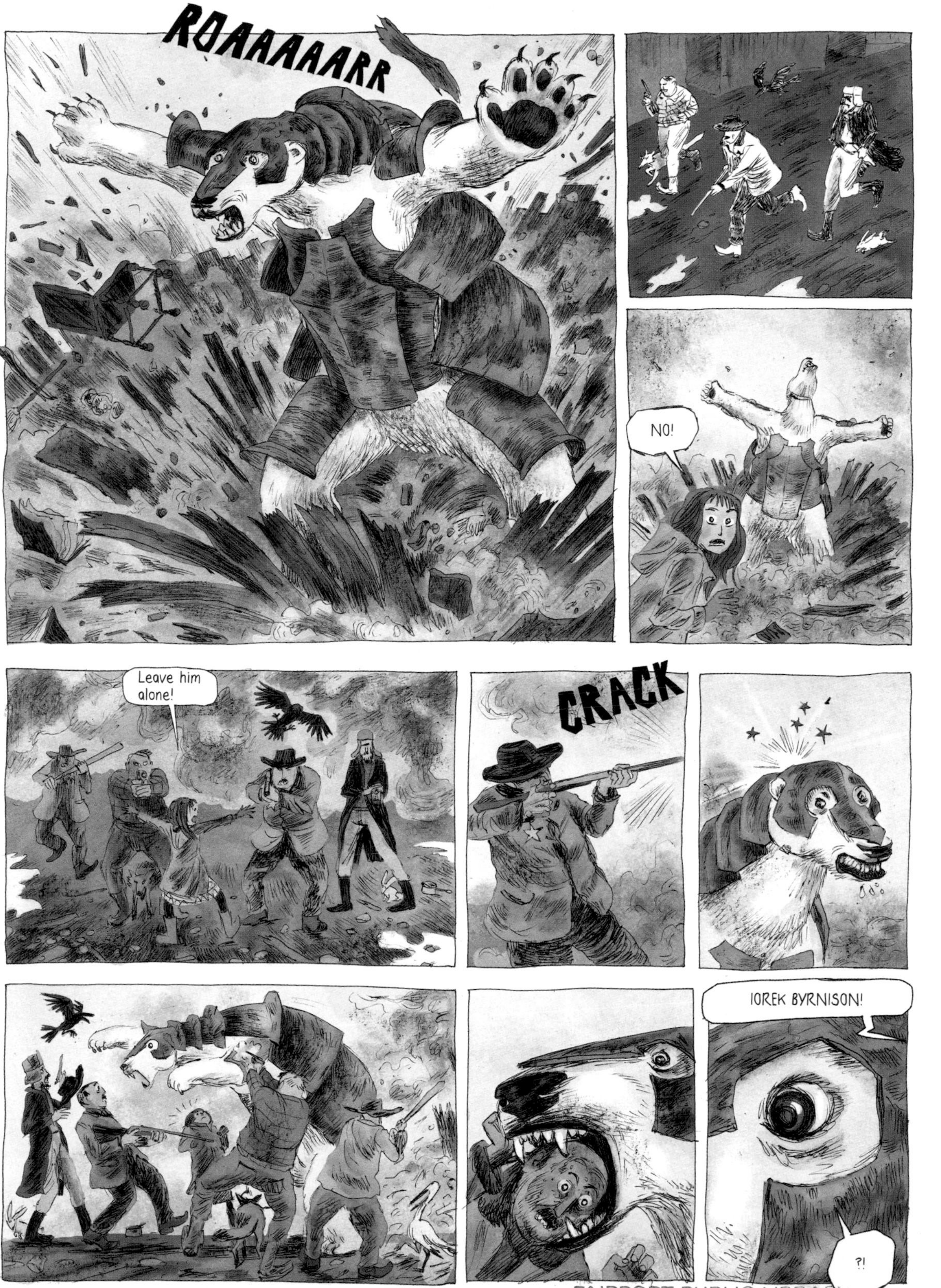
ROAAAAAARR
NO!
Leave him alone!
CRACK
IOREK BYRNISON!
?!

882

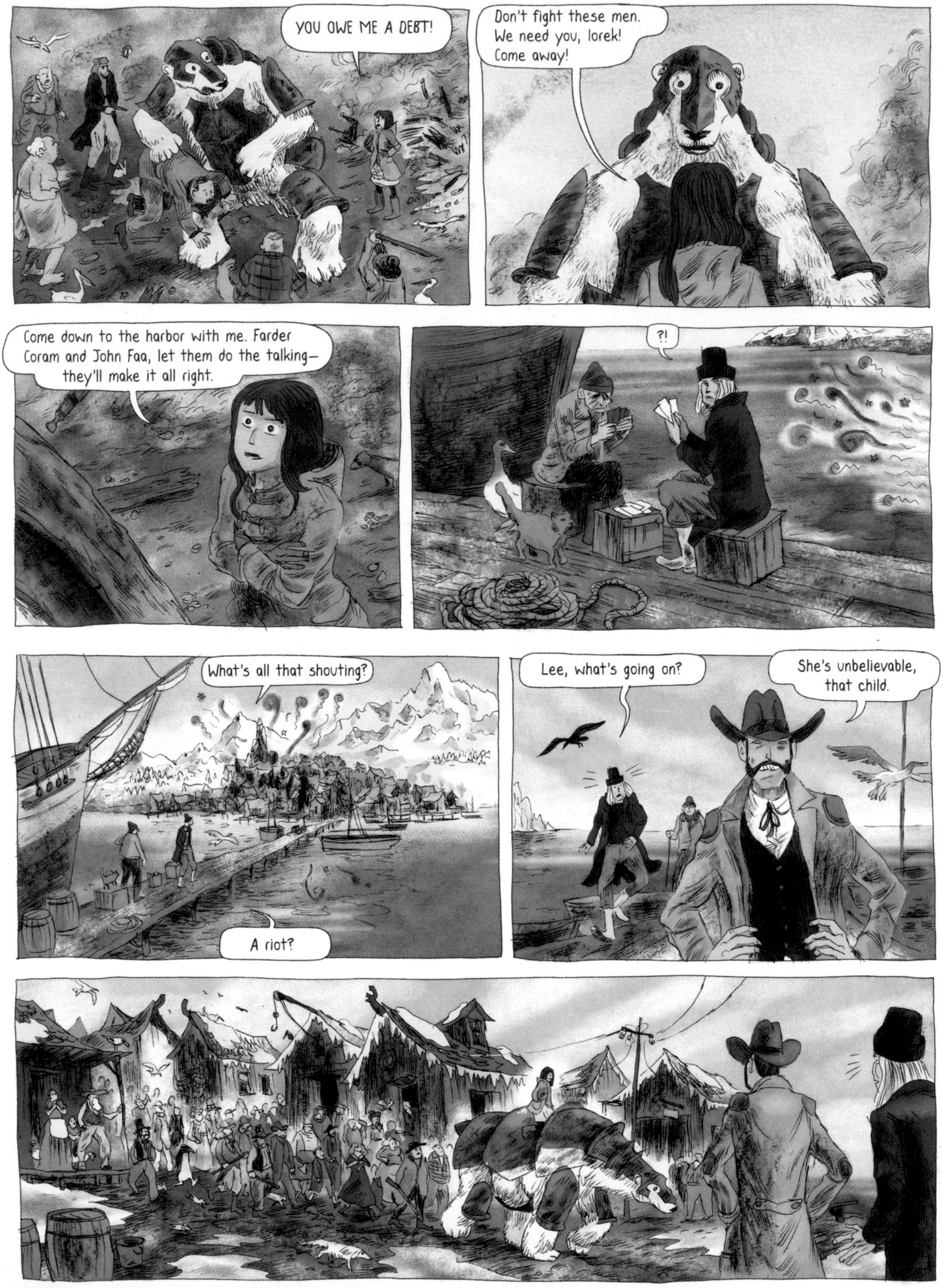
YOU OWE ME A DEBT!
Don't fight these men. We need you, Iorek! Come away!
Come down to the harbor with me. Farder Coram and John Faa, let them do the talking—they'll make it all right.
?!
What's all that shouting?
A riot?
Lee, what's going on?
She's unbelievable, that child.

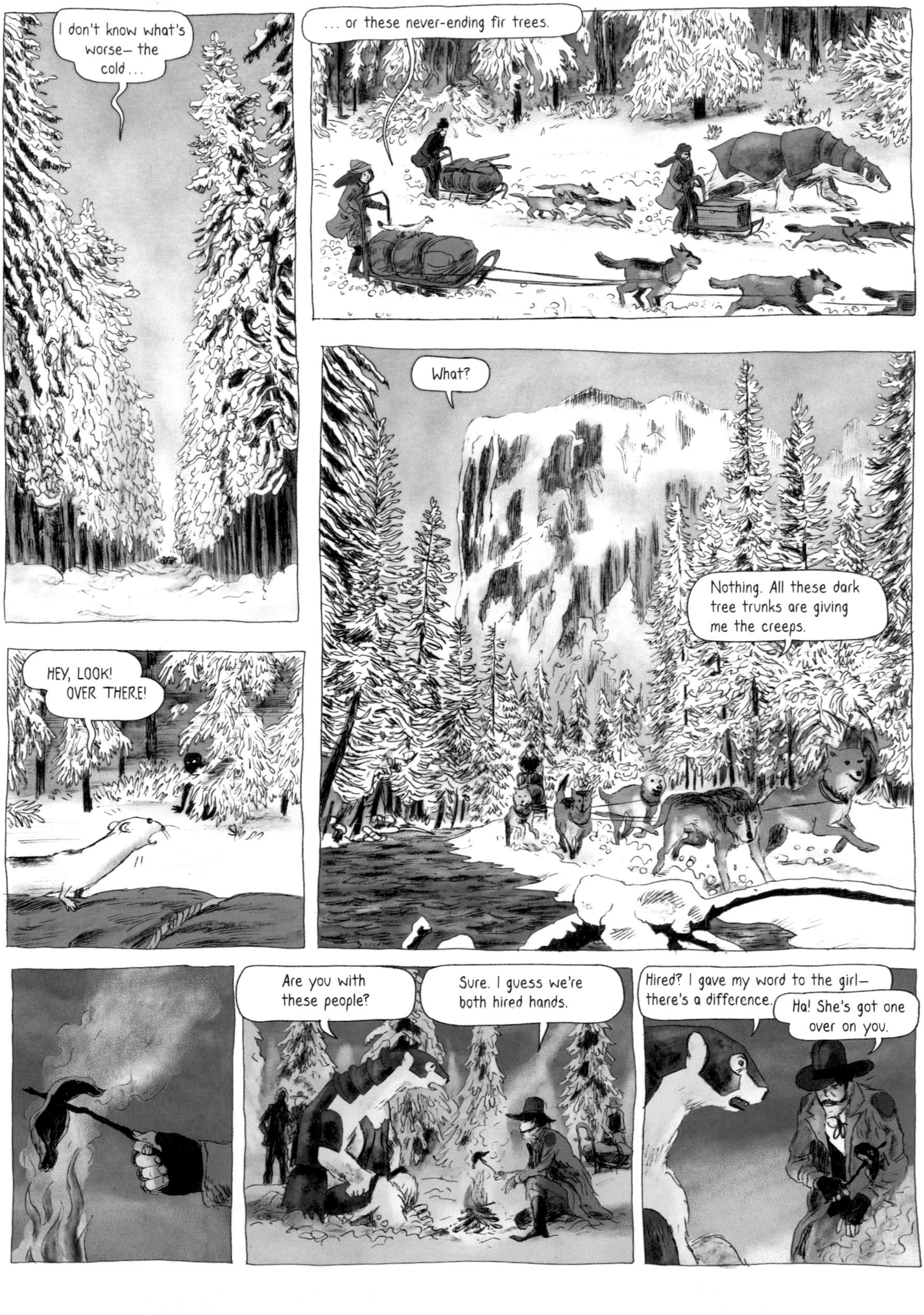
I don't know what's worse— the cold . . .
. . . or these never-ending fir trees.
HEY, LOOK! OVER THERE!
What?
Nothing. All these dark tree trunks are giving me the creeps.
Are you with these people?
Sure. I guess we're both hired hands.
Hired? I gave my word to the girl— there's a difference.
Ha! She's got one over on you.

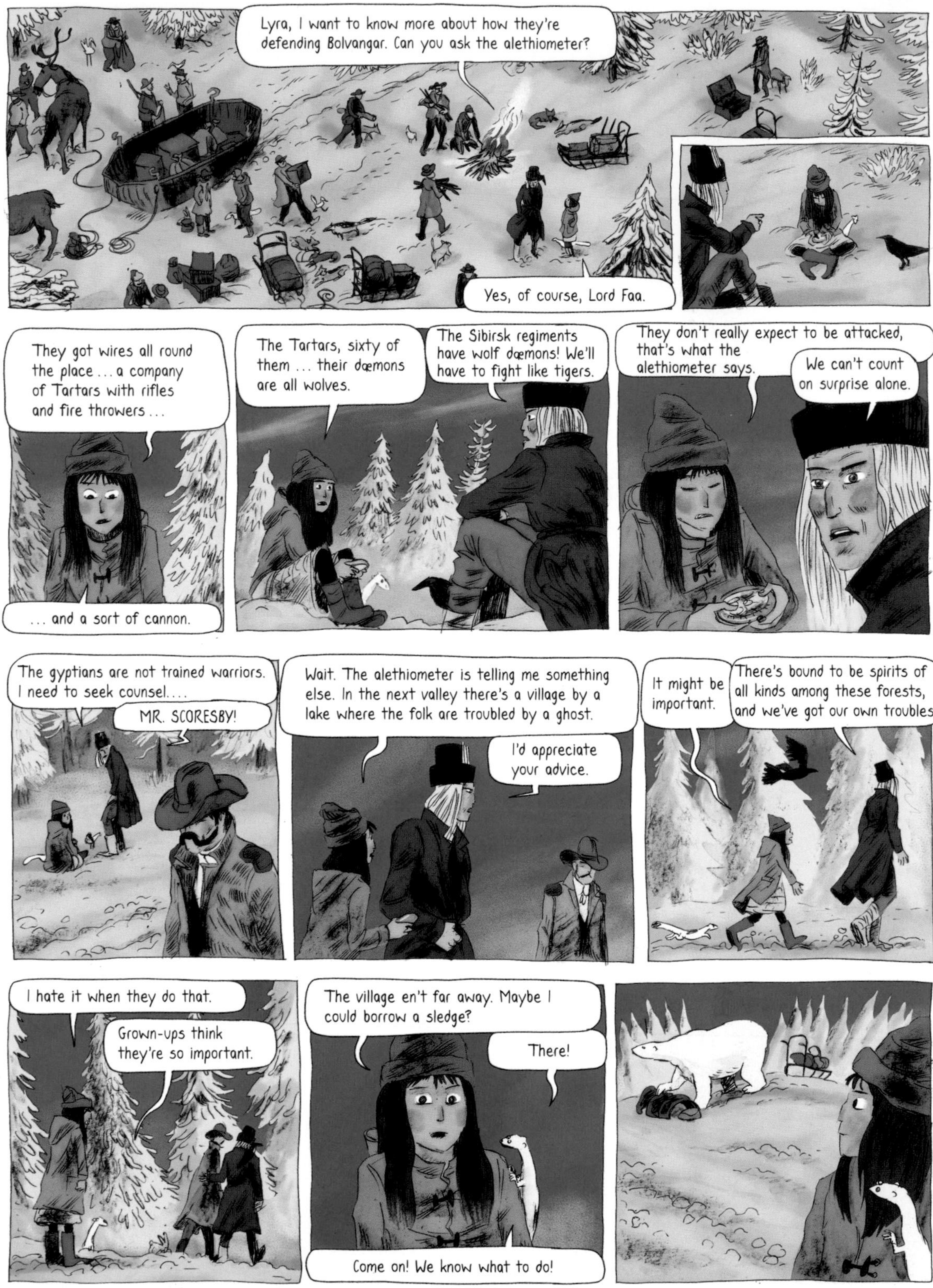

Lyra, I want to know more about how they're defending Bolvangar. Can you ask the alethiometer?
Yes, of course, Lord Faa.
They got wires all round the place . . . a company of Tartars with rifles and fire throwers . . .
. . . and a sort of cannon.
The Tartars, sixty of them . . . their dæmons are all wolves.
The Sibirsk regiments have wolf dæmons! We'll have to fight like tigers.
They don't really expect to be attacked, that's what the alethiometer says.
We can't count on surprise alone.
The gyptians are not trained warriors. I need to seek counsel. . . .
MR. SCORESBY!
Wait. The alethiometer is telling me something else. In the next valley there's a village by a lake where the folk are troubled by a ghost.
I'd appreciate your advice.
It might be important.
There's bound to be spirits of all kinds among these forests, and we've got our own troubles.
I hate it when they do that.
Grown-ups think they're so important.
The village en't far away. Maybe I could borrow a sledge?
There!
Come on! We know what to do!

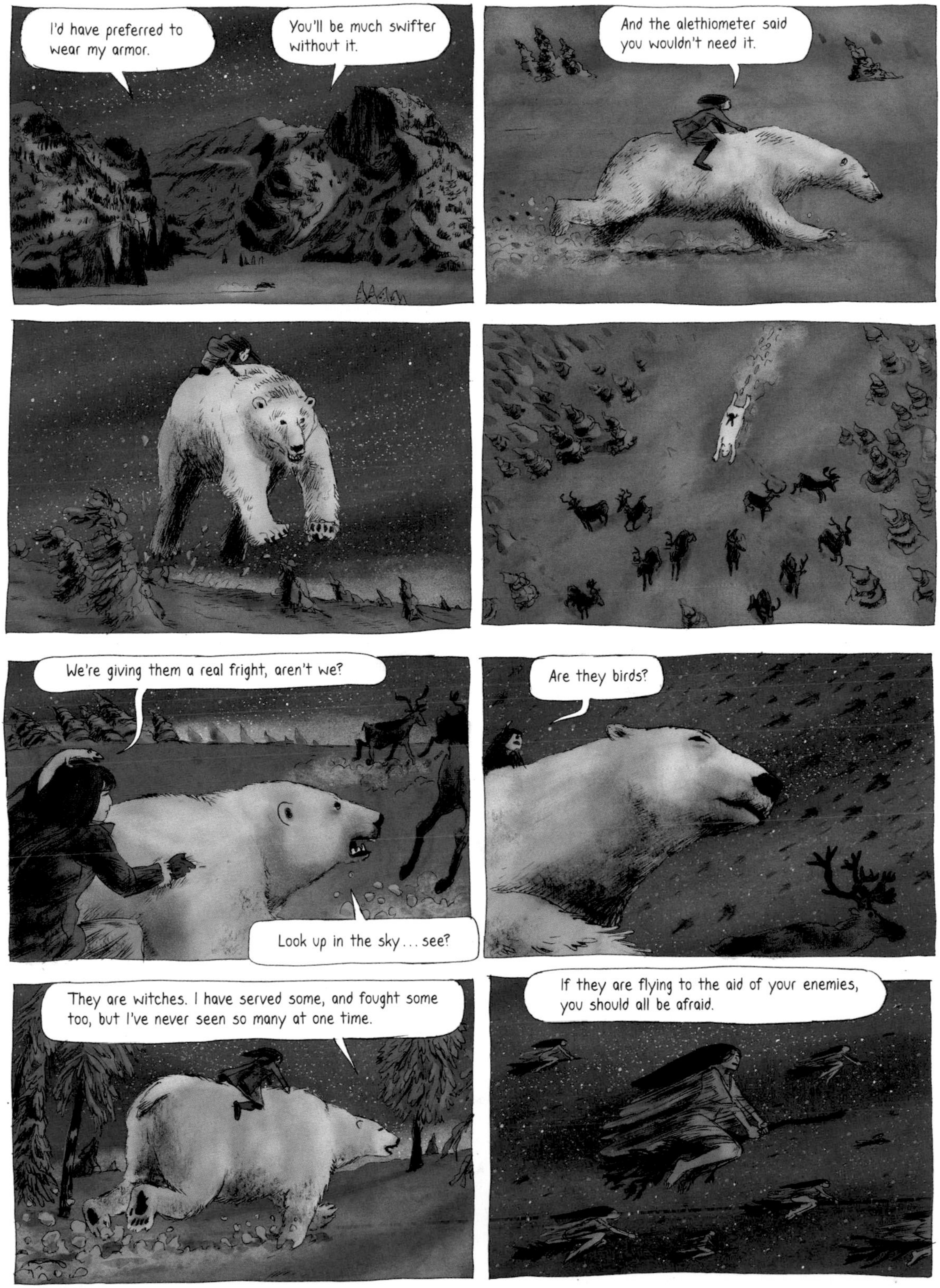
I'd have preferred to wear my armor.
You'll be much swifter without it.
And the alethiometer said you wouldn't need it.
We're giving them a real fright, aren't we?
Look up in the sky... see?
Are they birds?
They are witches. I have served some, and fought some too, but I've never seen so many at one time.
If they are flying to the aid of your enemies, you should all be afraid.

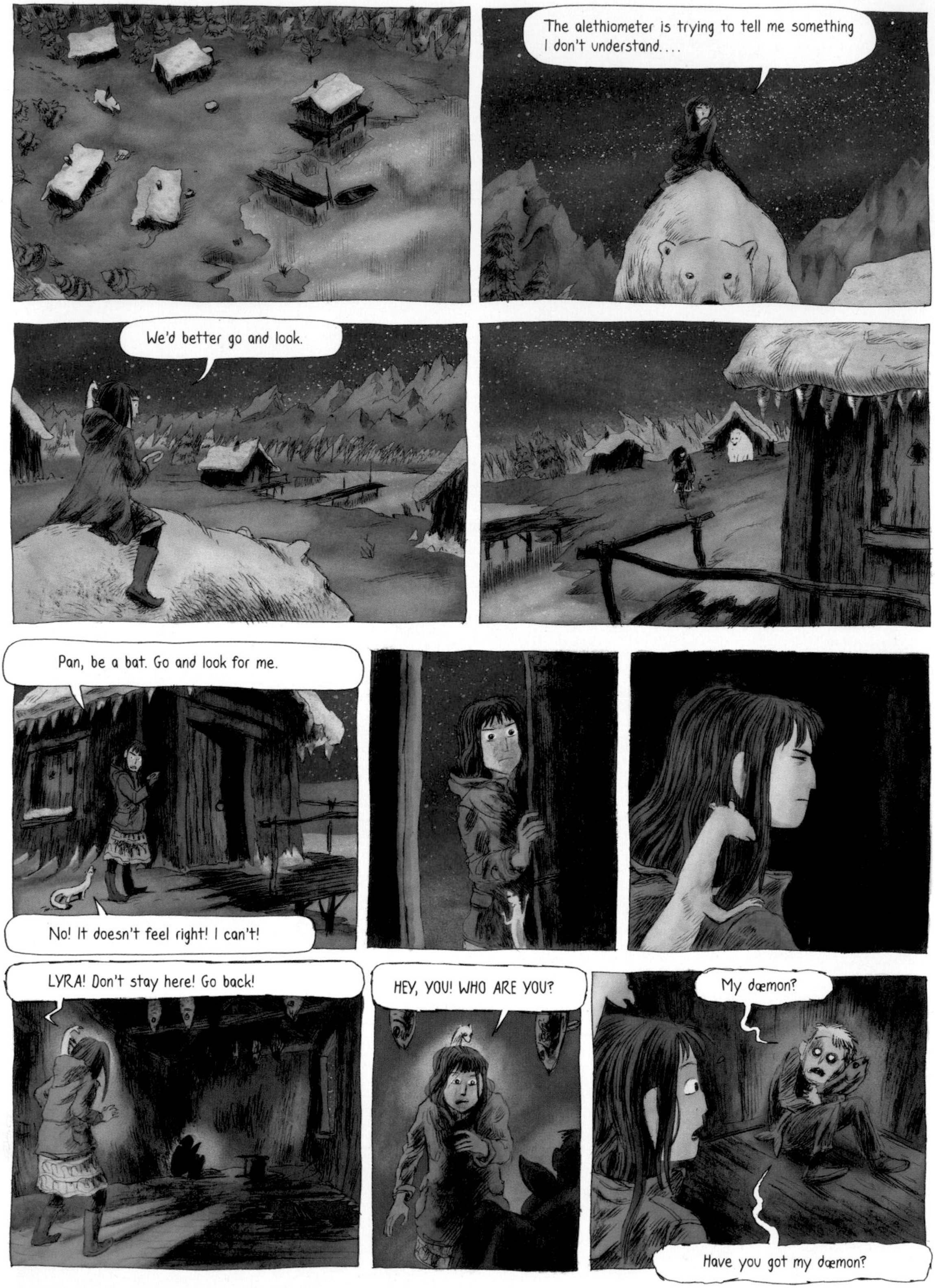
The alethiometer is trying to tell me something I don't understand....
We'd better go and look.
Pan, be a bat. Go and look for me.
No! It doesn't feel right! I can't!
LYRA! Don't stay here! Go back!
HEY, YOU! WHO ARE YOU?
My dæmon?
Have you got my dæmon?

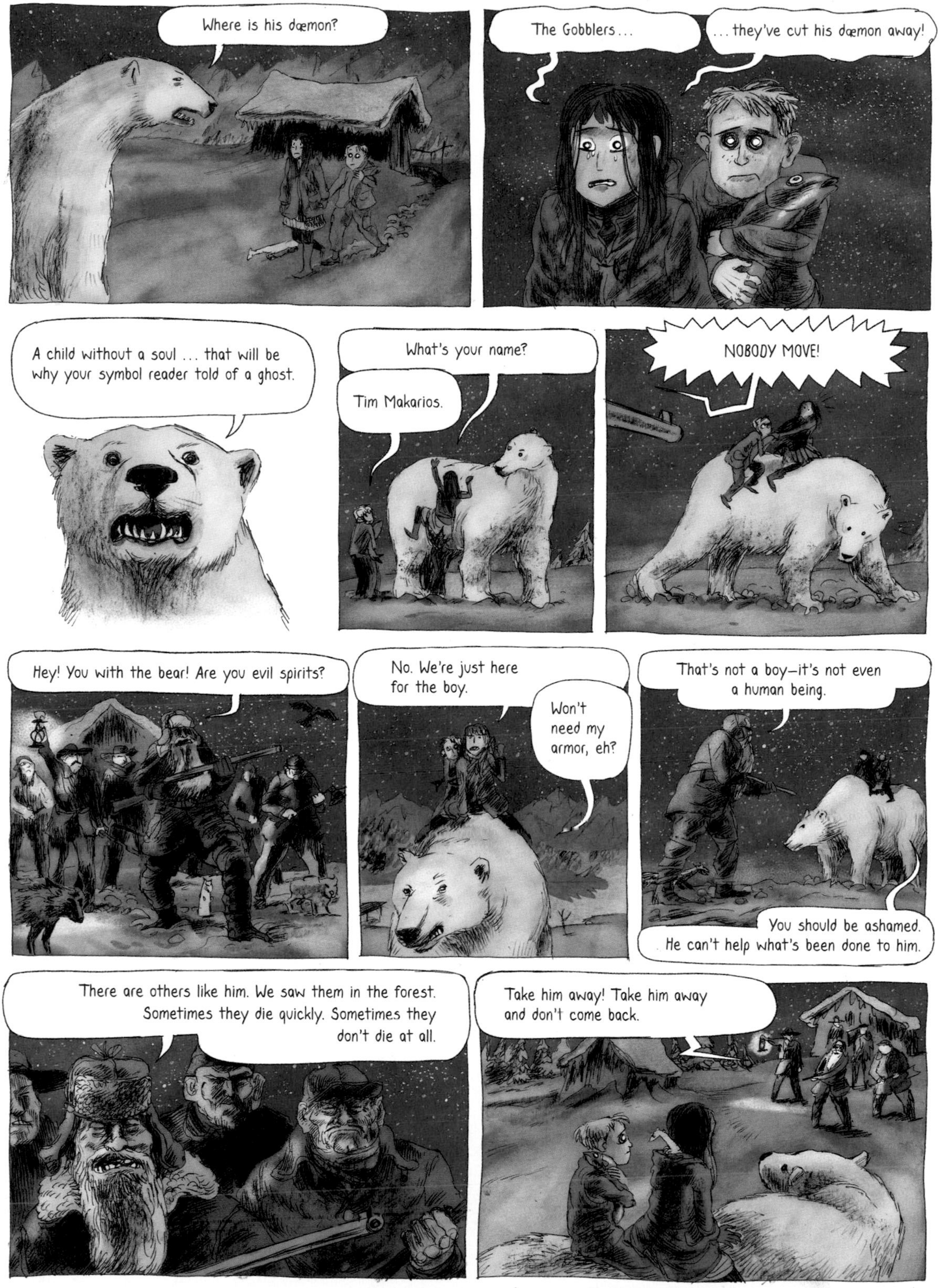
Where is his dæmon?
The Gobblers...
...they've cut his dæmon away!
A child without a soul ... that will be why your symbol reader told of a ghost.
What's your name?
Tim Makarios.
NOBODY MOVE!
Hey! You with the bear! Are you evil spirits?
No. We're just here for the boy.
Won't need my armor, eh?
That's not a boy—it's not even a human being.
You should be ashamed. He can't help what's been done to him.
There are others like him. We saw them in the forest. Sometimes they die quickly. Sometimes they don't die at all.
Take him away! Take him away and don't come back.

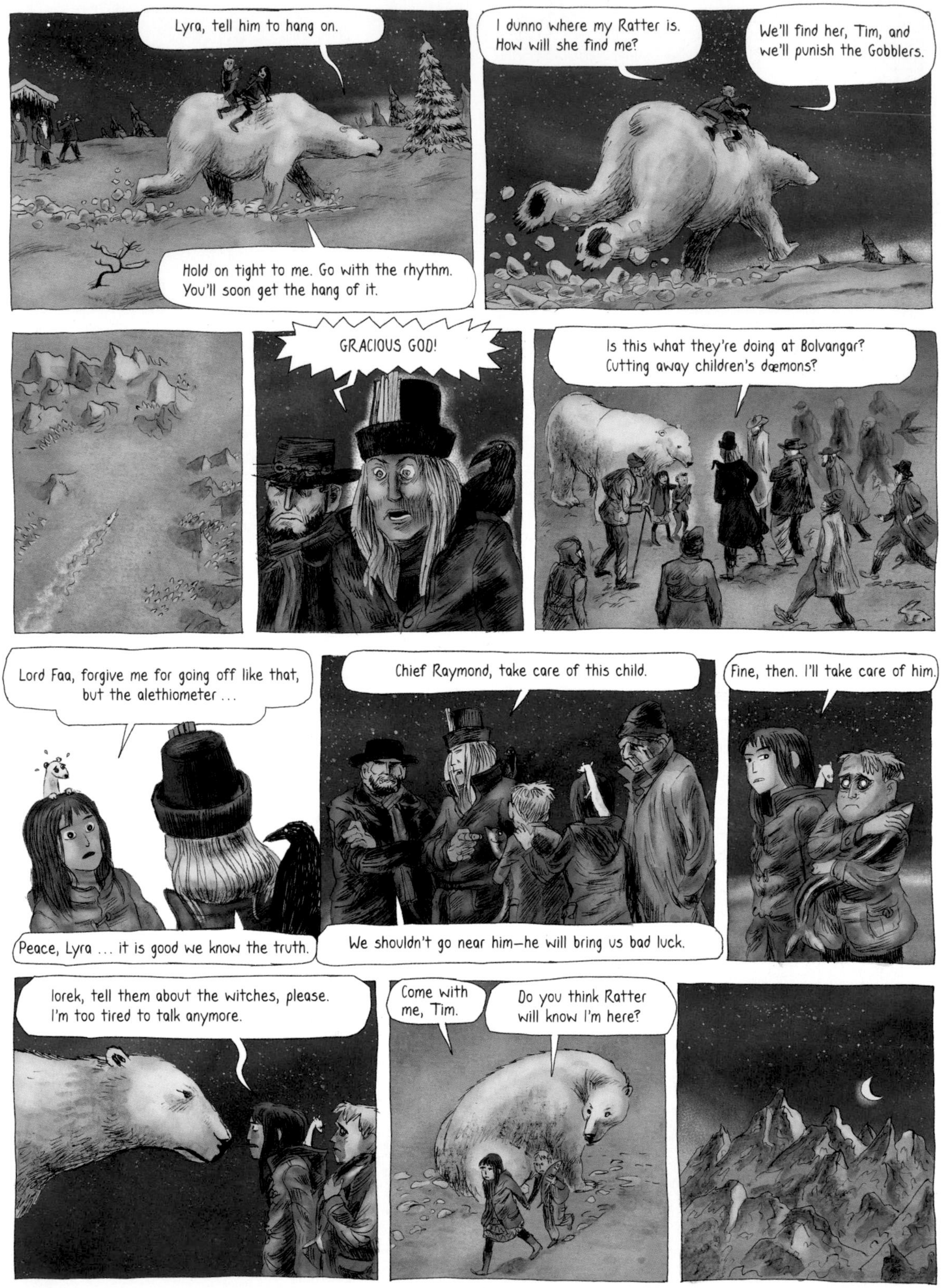
Lyra, tell him to hang on.
Hold on tight to me. Go with the rhythm. You'll soon get the hang of it.
I dunno where my Ratter is. How will she find me?
We'll find her, Tim, and we'll punish the Gobblers.
GRACIOUS GOD!
Is this what they're doing at Bolvangar? Cutting away children's dæmons?
Lord Faa, forgive me for going off like that, but the alethiometer . . .
Peace, Lyra . . . it is good we know the truth.
Chief Raymond, take care of this child.
We shouldn't go near him—he will bring us bad luck.
Fine, then. I'll take care of him.
Iorek, tell them about the witches, please. I'm too tired to talk anymore.
Come with me, Tim.
Do you think Ratter will know I'm here?

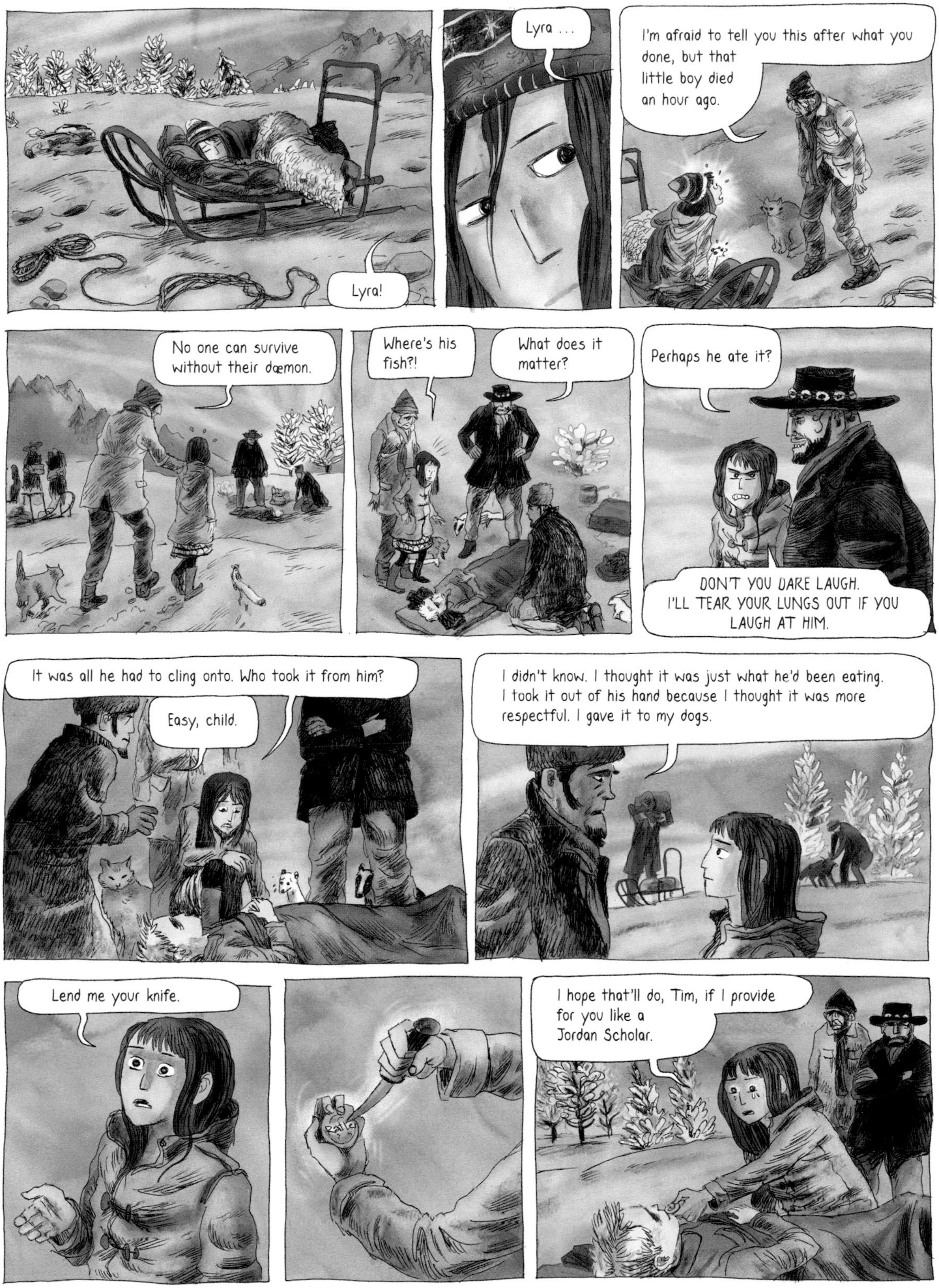
Lyra!
Lyra . . .
I'm afraid to tell you this after what you done, but that little boy died an hour ago.
No one can survive without their dæmon.
Where's his fish?!
What does it matter?
Perhaps he ate it?
DON'T YOU DARE LAUGH. I'LL TEAR YOUR LUNGS OUT IF YOU LAUGH AT HIM.
It was all he had to cling onto. Who took it from him?
Easy, child.
I didn't know. I thought it was just what he'd been eating. I took it out of his hand because I thought it was more respectful. I gave it to my dogs.
Lend me your knife.
Ratter
I hope that'll do, Tim, if I provide for you like a Jordan Scholar.

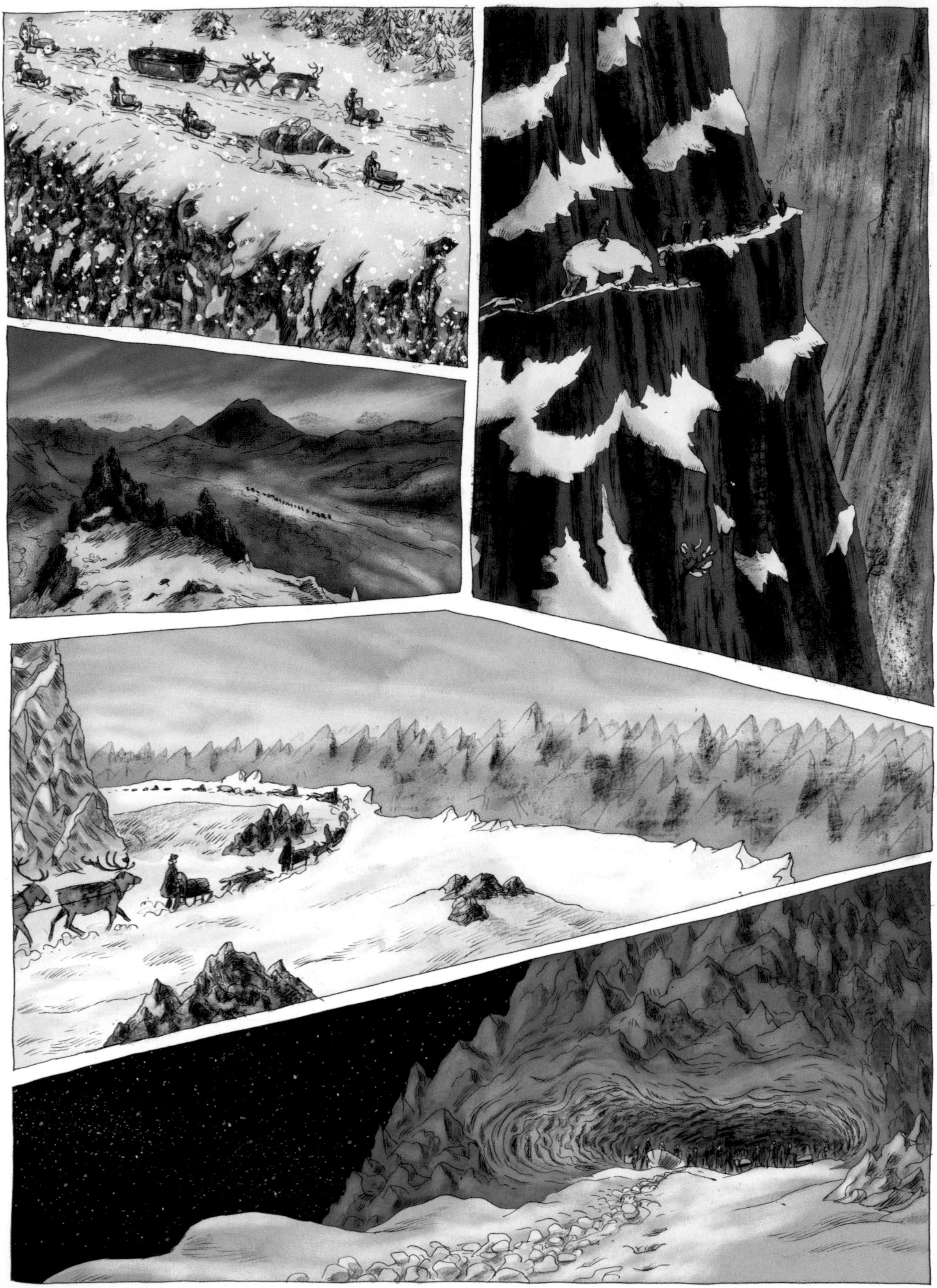

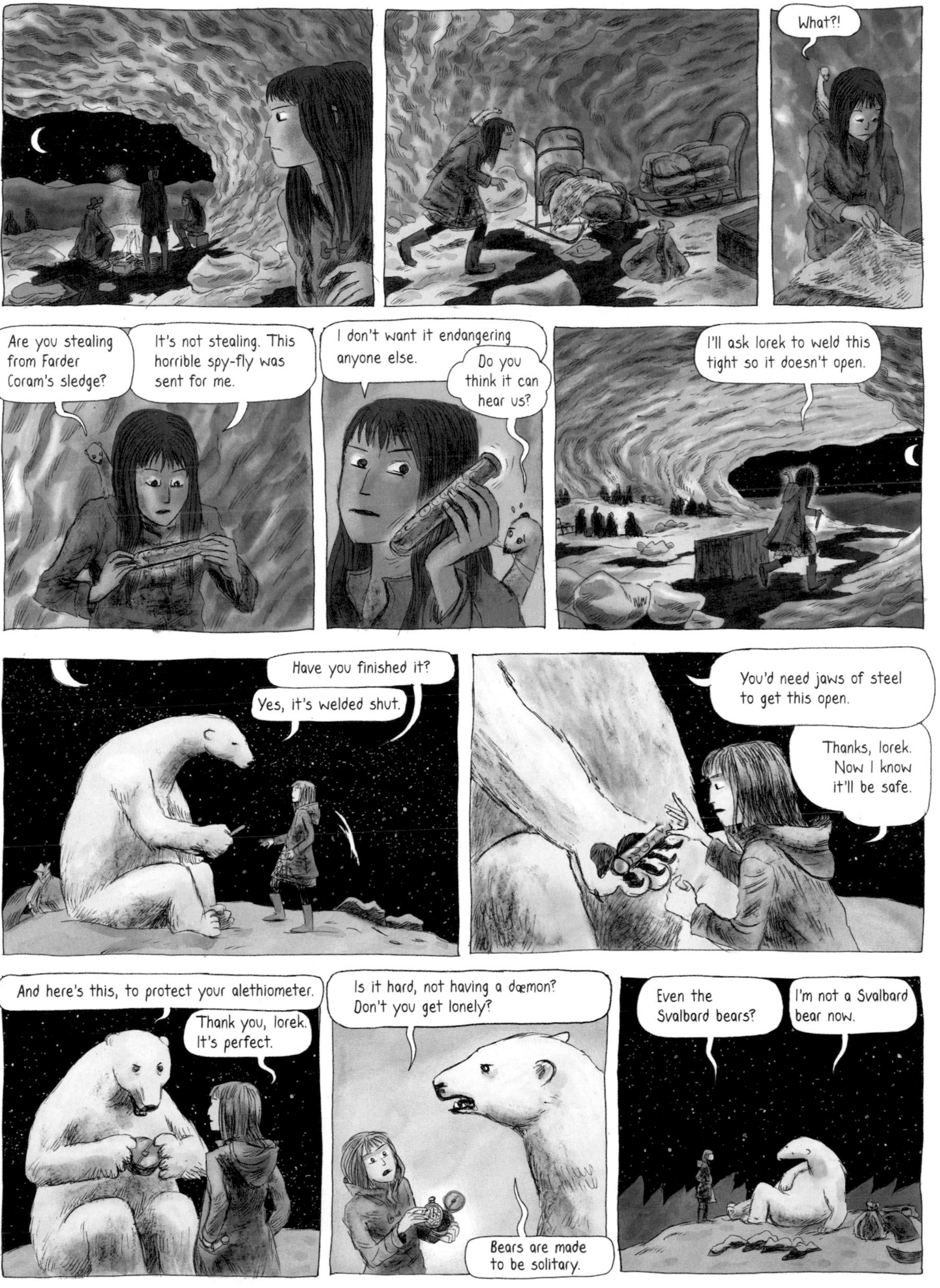
What?!
Are you stealing from Farder Coram's sledge?
It's not stealing. This horrible spy-fly was sent for me.
I don't want it endangering anyone else.
Do you think it can hear us?
I'll ask Iorek to weld this tight so it doesn't open.
Have you finished it?
Yes, it's welded shut.
You'd need jaws of steel to get this open.
Thanks, Iorek. Now I know it'll be safe.
And here's this, to protect your alethiometer.
Thank you, Iorek. It's perfect.
Is it hard, not having a dæmon? Don't you get lonely?
Bears are made to be solitary.
Even the Svalbard bears?
I'm not a Svalbard bear now.

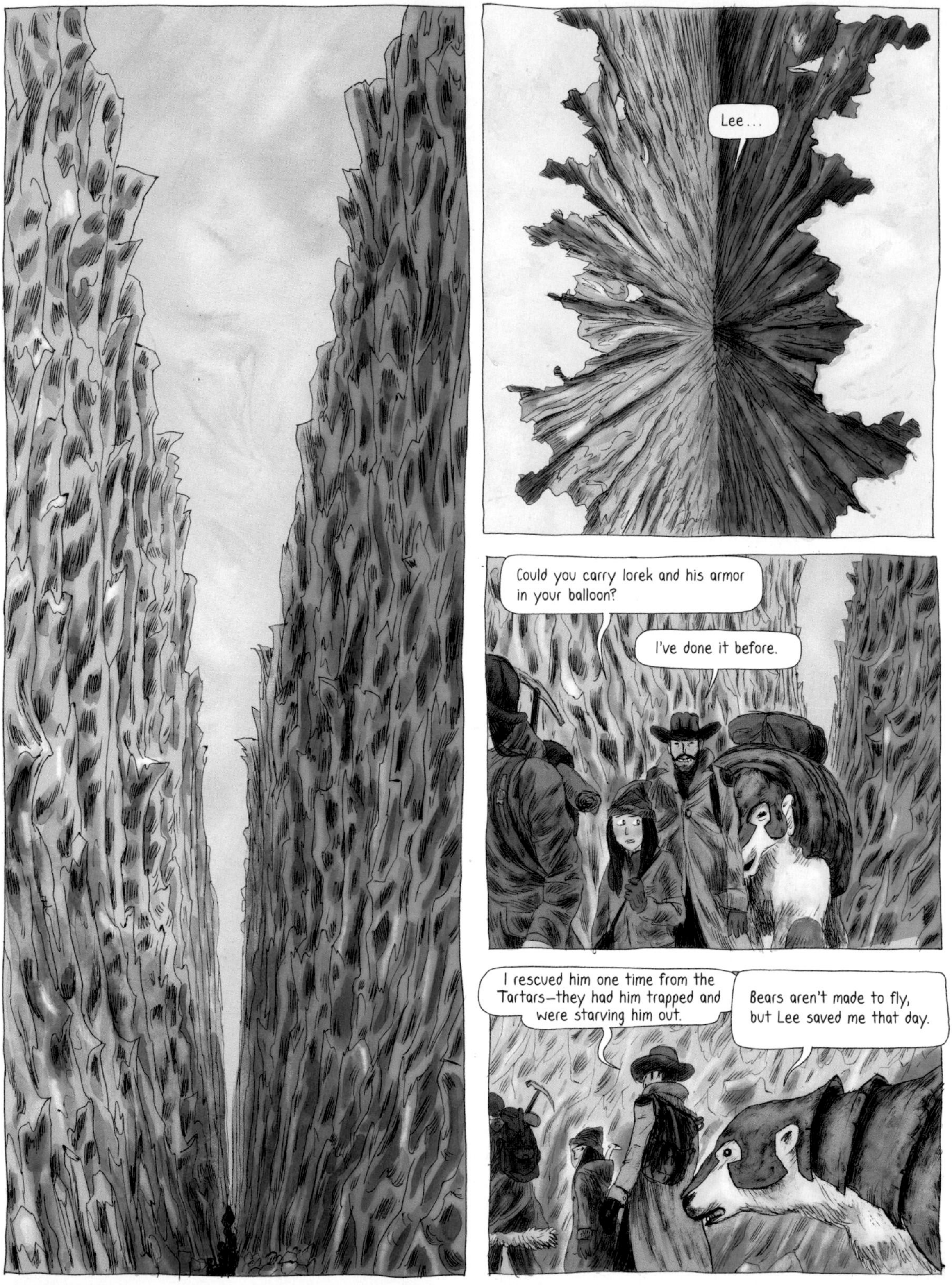
Lee...
Could you carry Iorek and his armor in your balloon?
I've done it before.
I rescued him one time from the Tartars—they had him trapped and were starving him out.
Bears aren't made to fly, but Lee saved me that day.

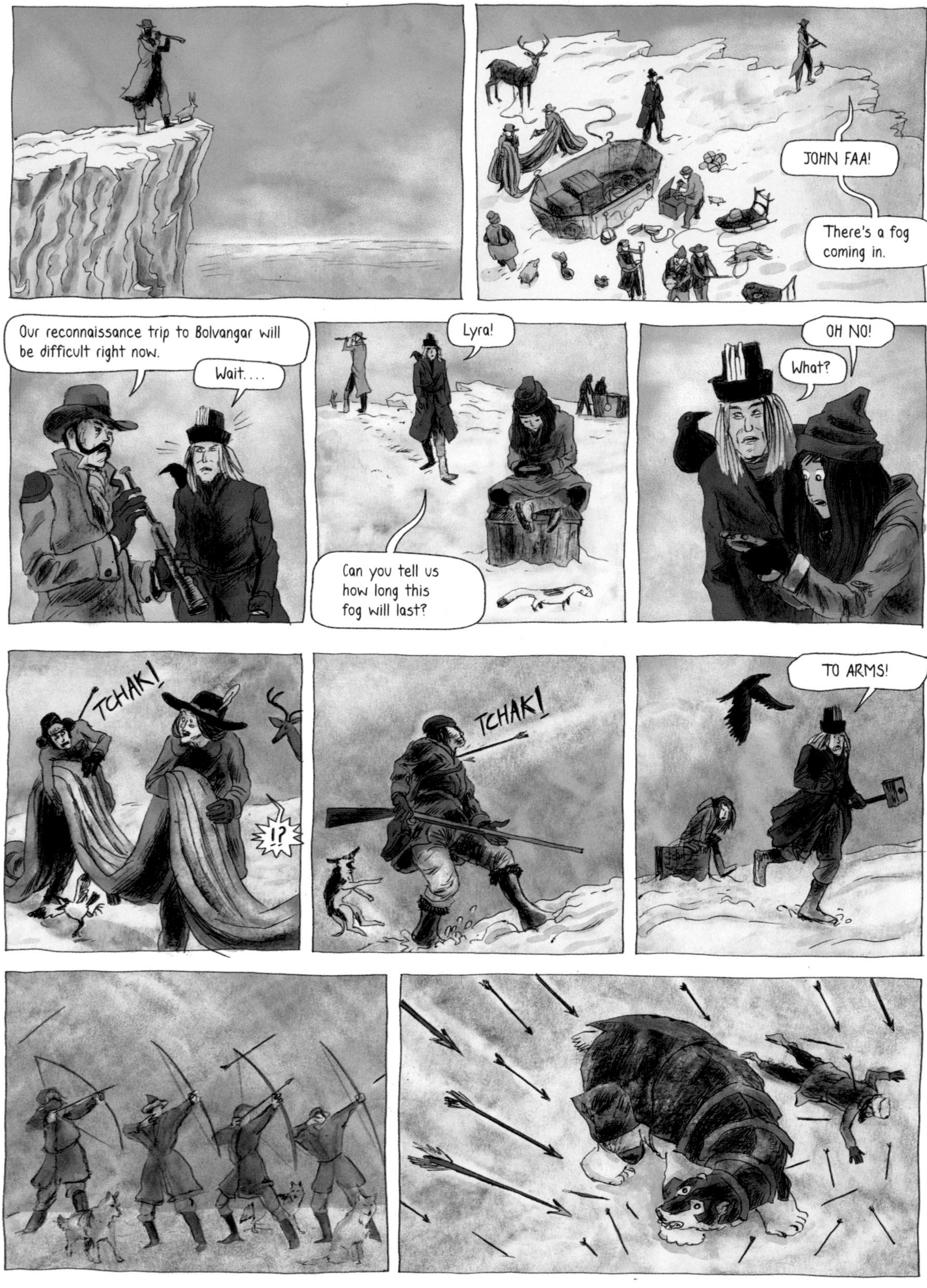
JOHN FAA!
There's a fog coming in.
Our reconnaissance trip to Bolvangar will be difficult right now.
Wait....
Lyra!
Can you tell us how long this fog will last?
OH NO!
What?
TCHAK!
!?
TCHAK!
TO ARMS!

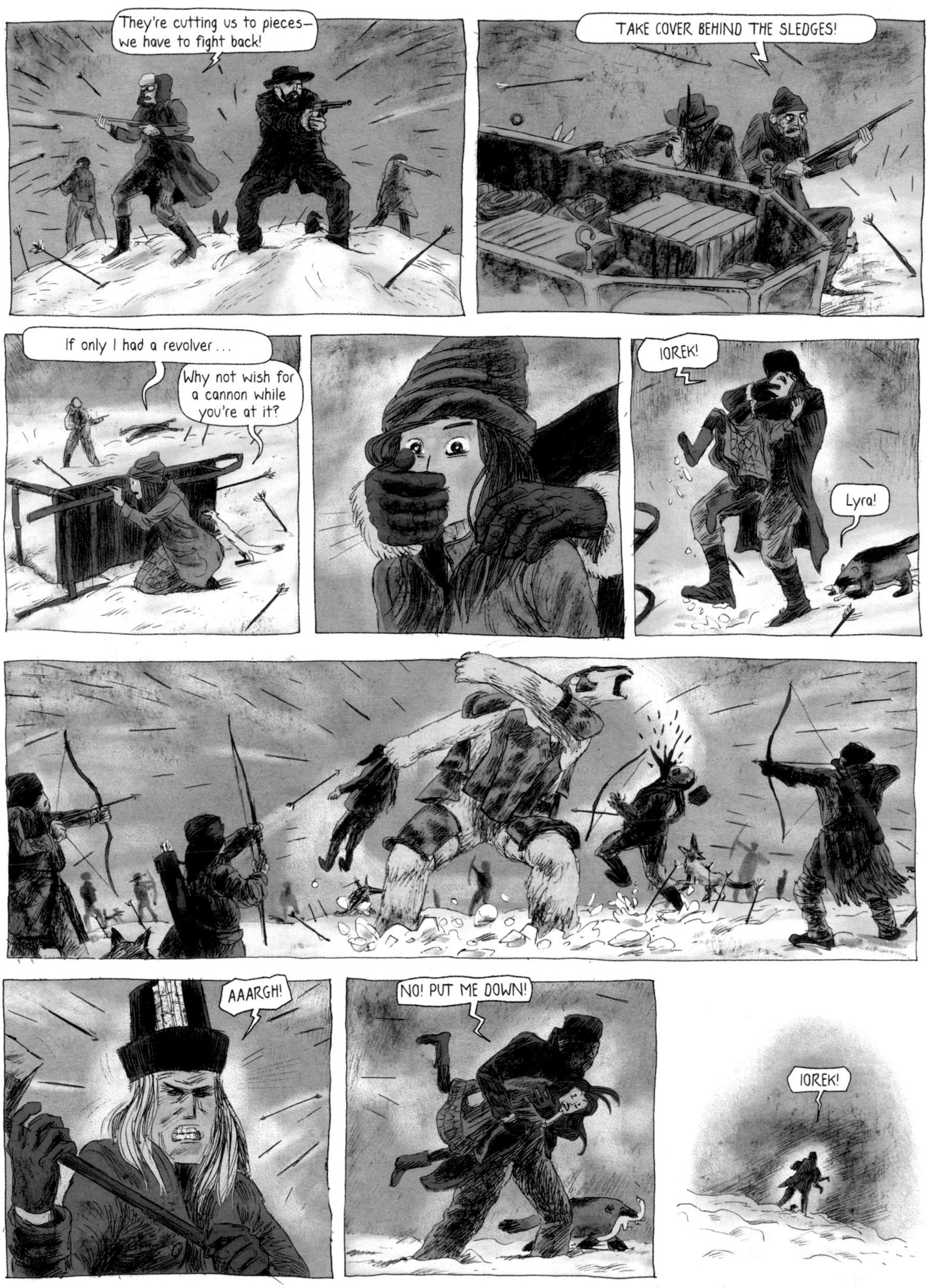
They're cutting us to pieces—we have to fight back!
TAKE COVER BEHIND THE SLEDGES!
If only I had a revolver . . .
Why not wish for a cannon while you're at it?
IOREK!
Lyra!
AAARGH!
NO! PUT ME DOWN!
IOREK!

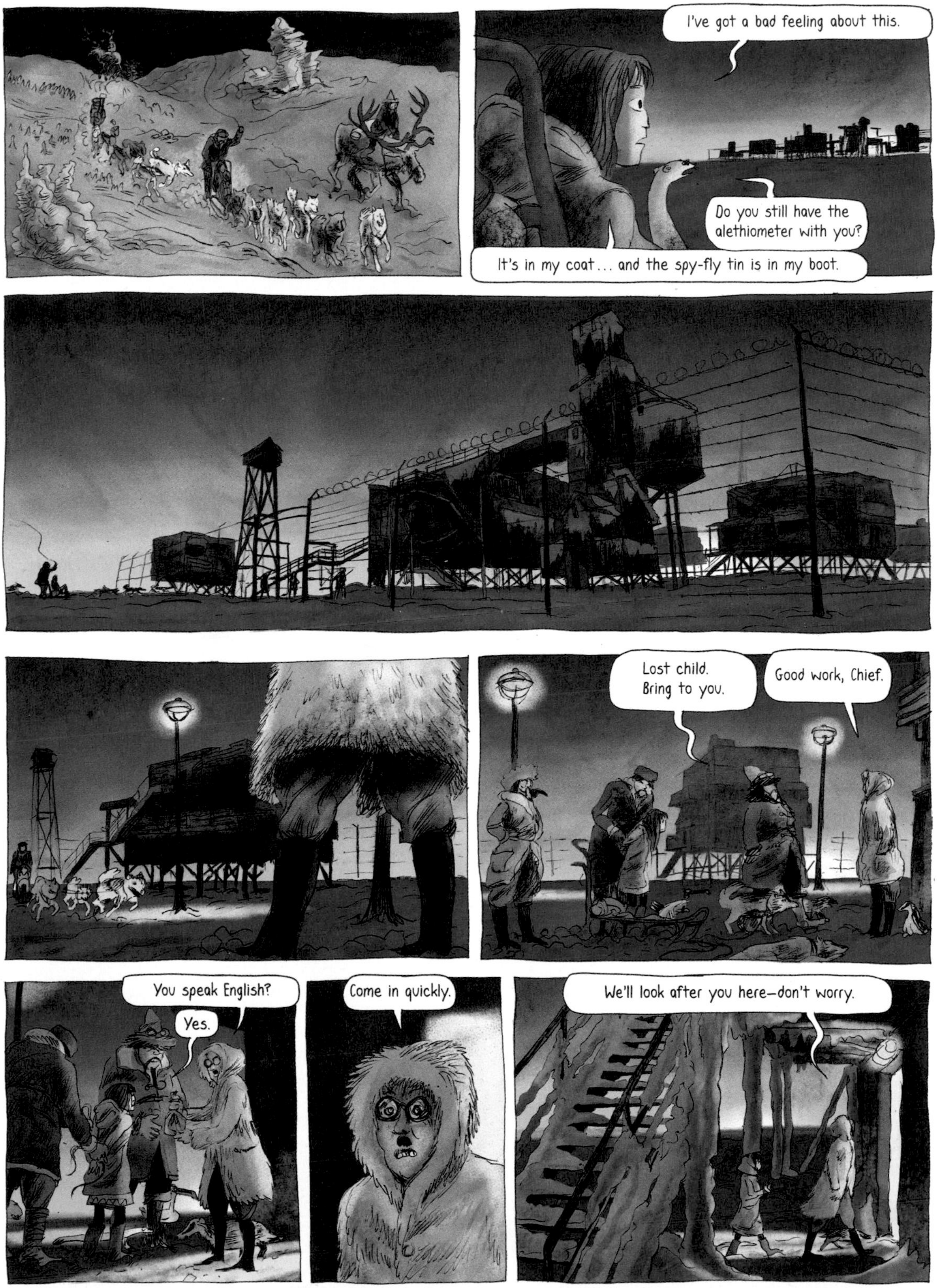
I've got a bad feeling about this.
Do you still have the alethiometer with you?
It's in my coat... and the spy-fly tin is in my boot.
Lost child. Bring to you.
Good work, Chief.
You speak English?
Yes.
Come in quickly.
We'll look after you here—don't worry.

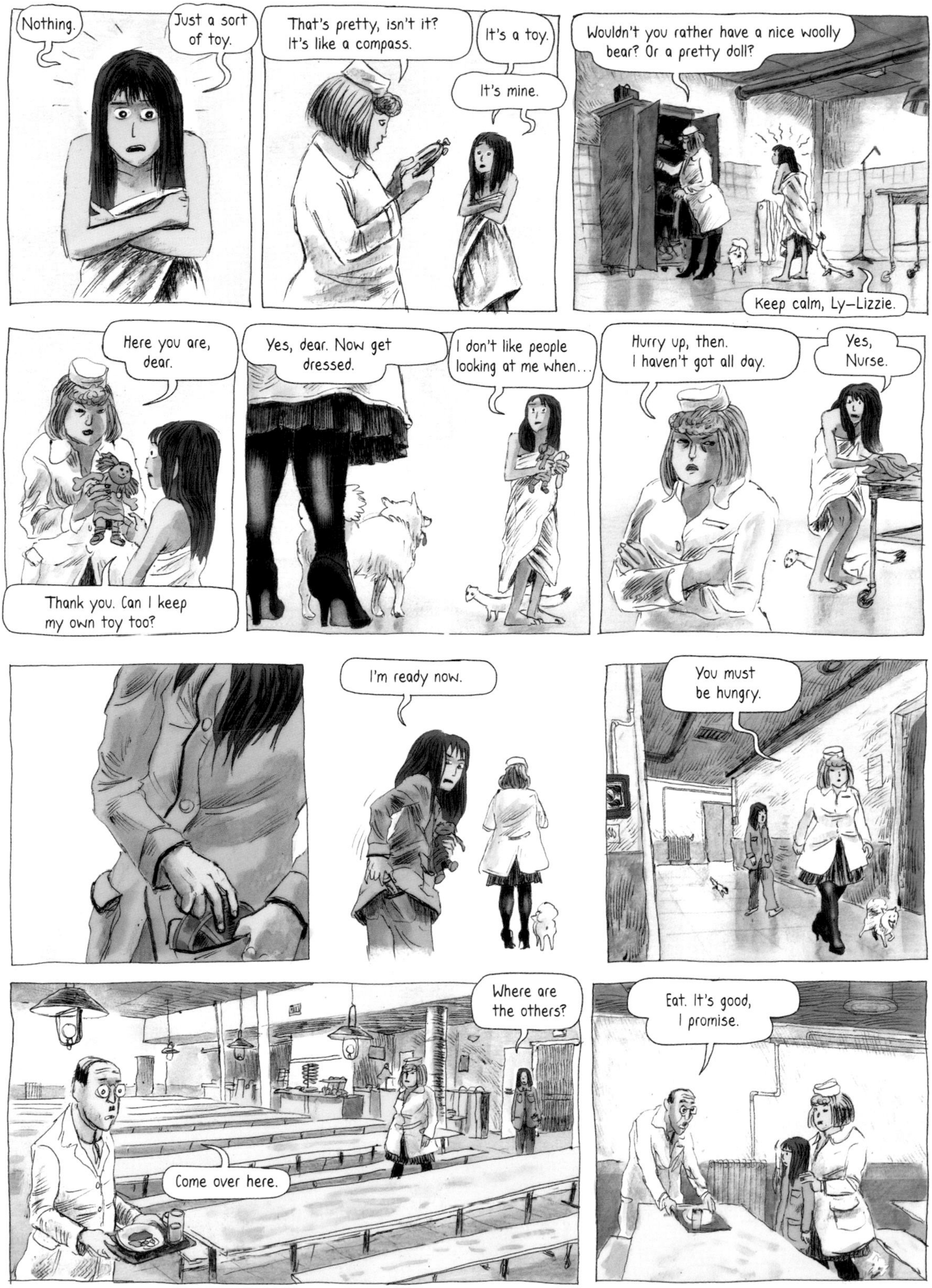
Nothing.
Just a sort of toy.
That's pretty, isn't it? It's like a compass.
It's a toy.
It's mine.
Wouldn't you rather have a nice woolly bear? Or a pretty doll?
Keep calm, Ly–Lizzie.
Here you are, dear.
Thank you. Can I keep my own toy too?
Yes, dear. Now get dressed.
I don't like people looking at me when...
Hurry up, then. I haven't got all day.
Yes, Nurse.
I'm ready now.
You must be hungry.
Where are the others?
Come over here.
Eat. It's good, I promise.

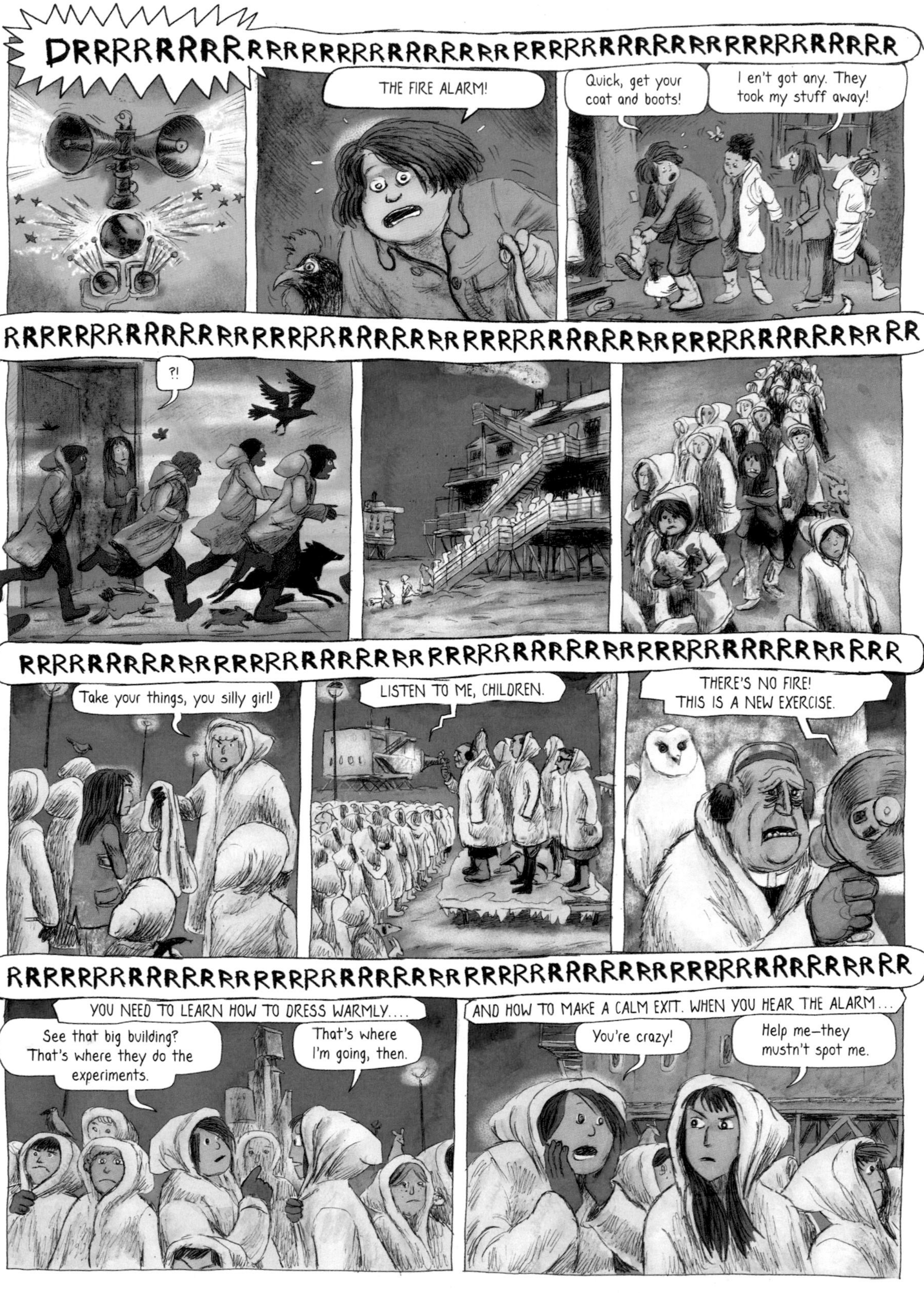
DRRRRRRRRRRRRRRRRRRRRRRRRRRRRRRRRRRRRRRRRRRRRRR
THE FIRE ALARM!
Quick, get your coat and boots!
I en't got any. They took my stuff away!
RRRRRRRRRRRRRRRRRRRRRRRRRRRRRRRRRRRRRRRRRRRRRRRRR
?!
RRRRRRRRRRRRRRRRRRRRRRRRRRRRRRRRRRRRRRRRRRRRRRRRR
Take your things, you silly girl!
LISTEN TO ME, CHILDREN.
THERE'S NO FIRE! THIS IS A NEW EXERCISE.
RRRRRRRRRRRRRRRRRRRRRRRRRRRRRRRRRRRRRRRRRRRRRRRRR
YOU NEED TO LEARN HOW TO DRESS WARMLY....
See that big building? That's where they do the experiments.
That's where I'm going, then.
AND HOW TO MAKE A CALM EXIT. WHEN YOU HEAR THE ALARM...
You're crazy!
Help me—they mustn't spot me.

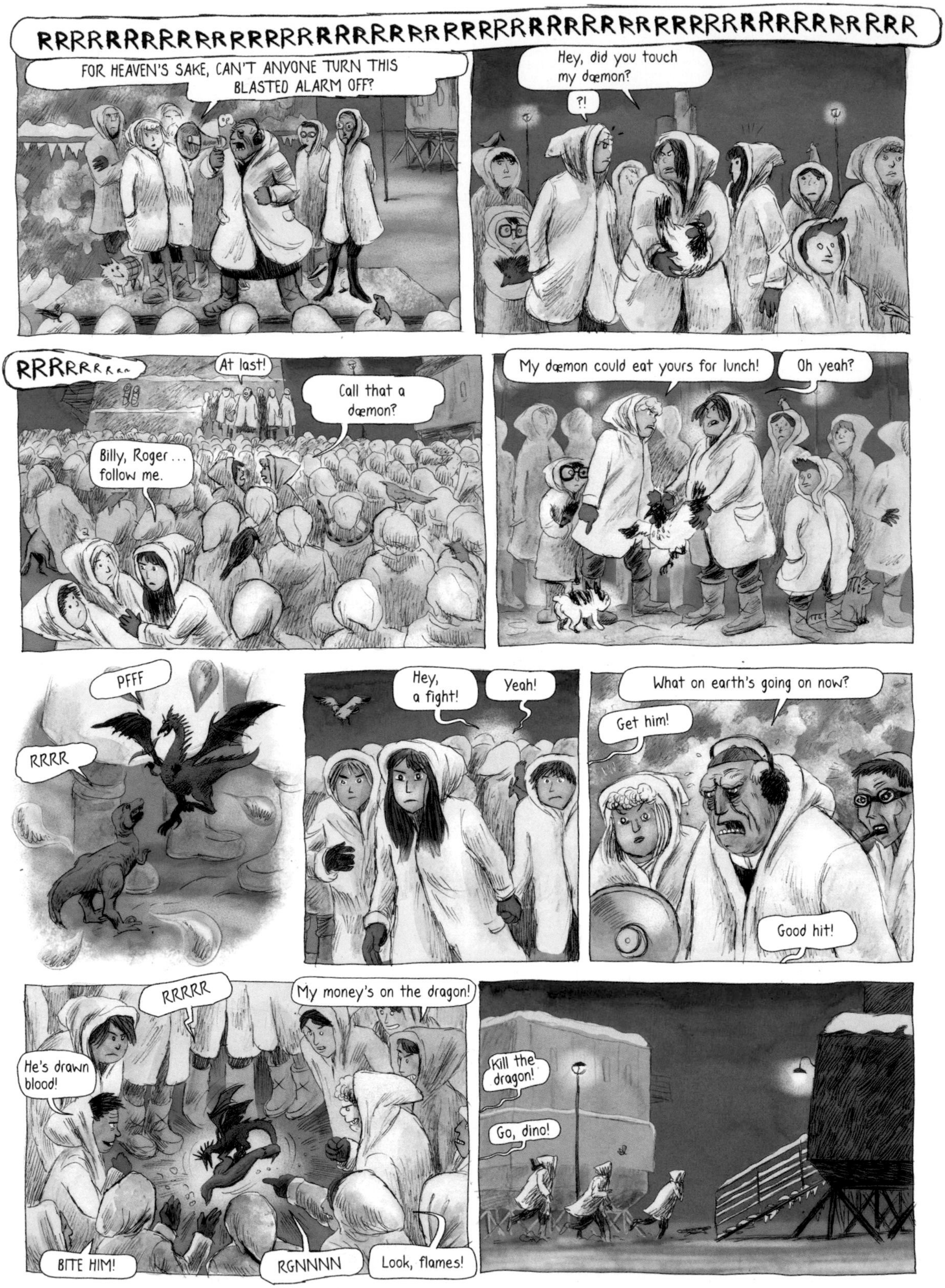
RRRRRRRRRRRRRRRRRRRRRRRRRRRRRRRRRRRRRRRRRRRRRRRRRR
FOR HEAVEN'S SAKE, CAN'T ANYONE TURN THIS BLASTED ALARM OFF?
Hey, did you touch my dæmon?
?!
RRRRRRRR
At last!
Call that a dæmon?
Billy, Roger... follow me.
My dæmon could eat yours for lunch!
Oh yeah?
PFFF
RRRR
Hey, a fight!
Yeah!
What on earth's going on now?
Get him!
Good hit!
RRRRR
My money's on the dragon!
He's drawn blood!
BITE HIM!
RGNNNN
Look, flames!
Kill the dragon!
Go, dino!

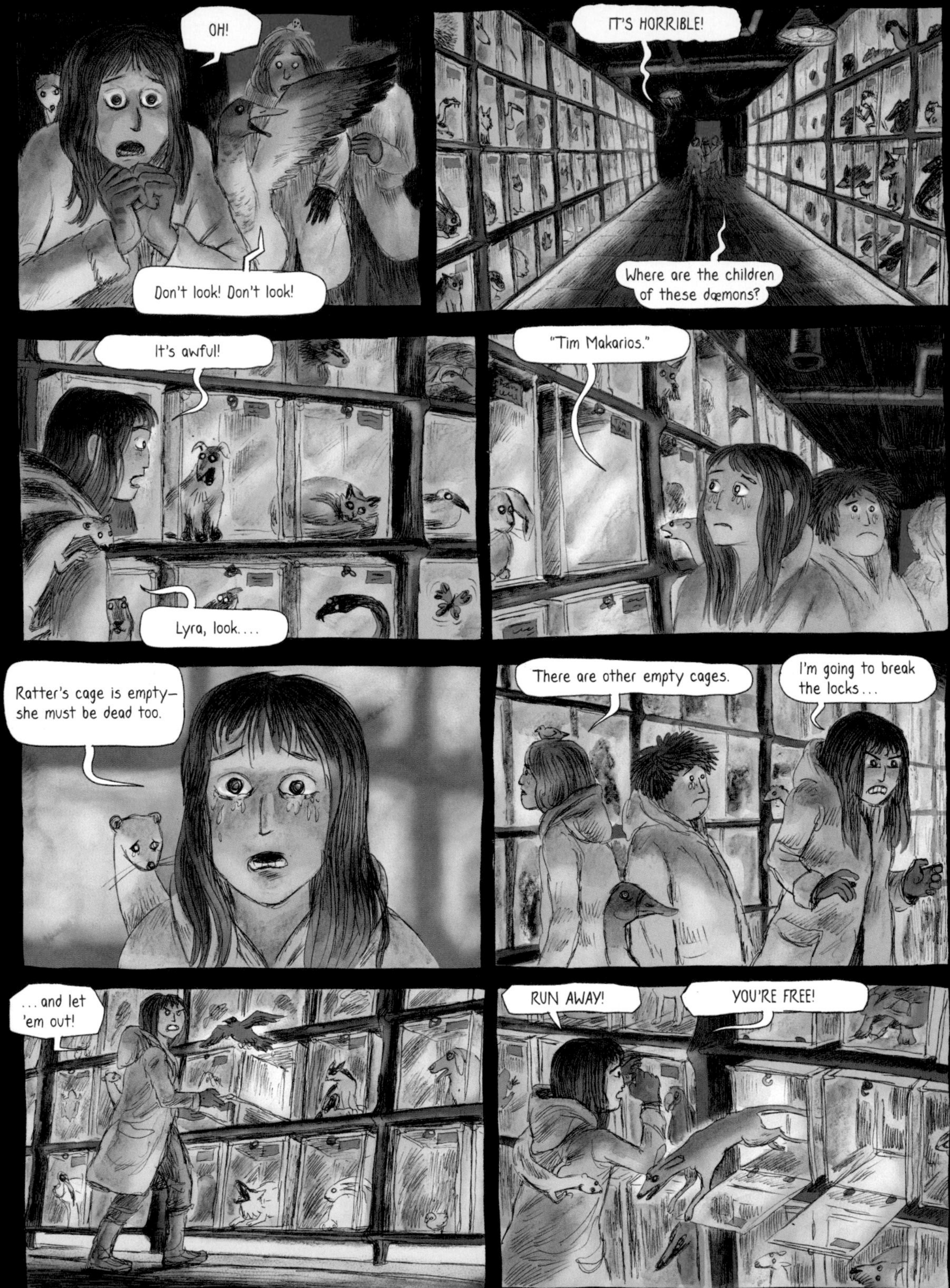
OH!
Don't look! Don't look!
IT'S HORRIBLE!
Where are the children of these dæmons?
It's awful!
Lyra, look. . . .
"Tim Makarios."
Ratter's cage is empty—she must be dead too.
There are other empty cages.
I'm going to break the locks . . .
. . . and let 'em out!
RUN AWAY!
YOU'RE FREE!

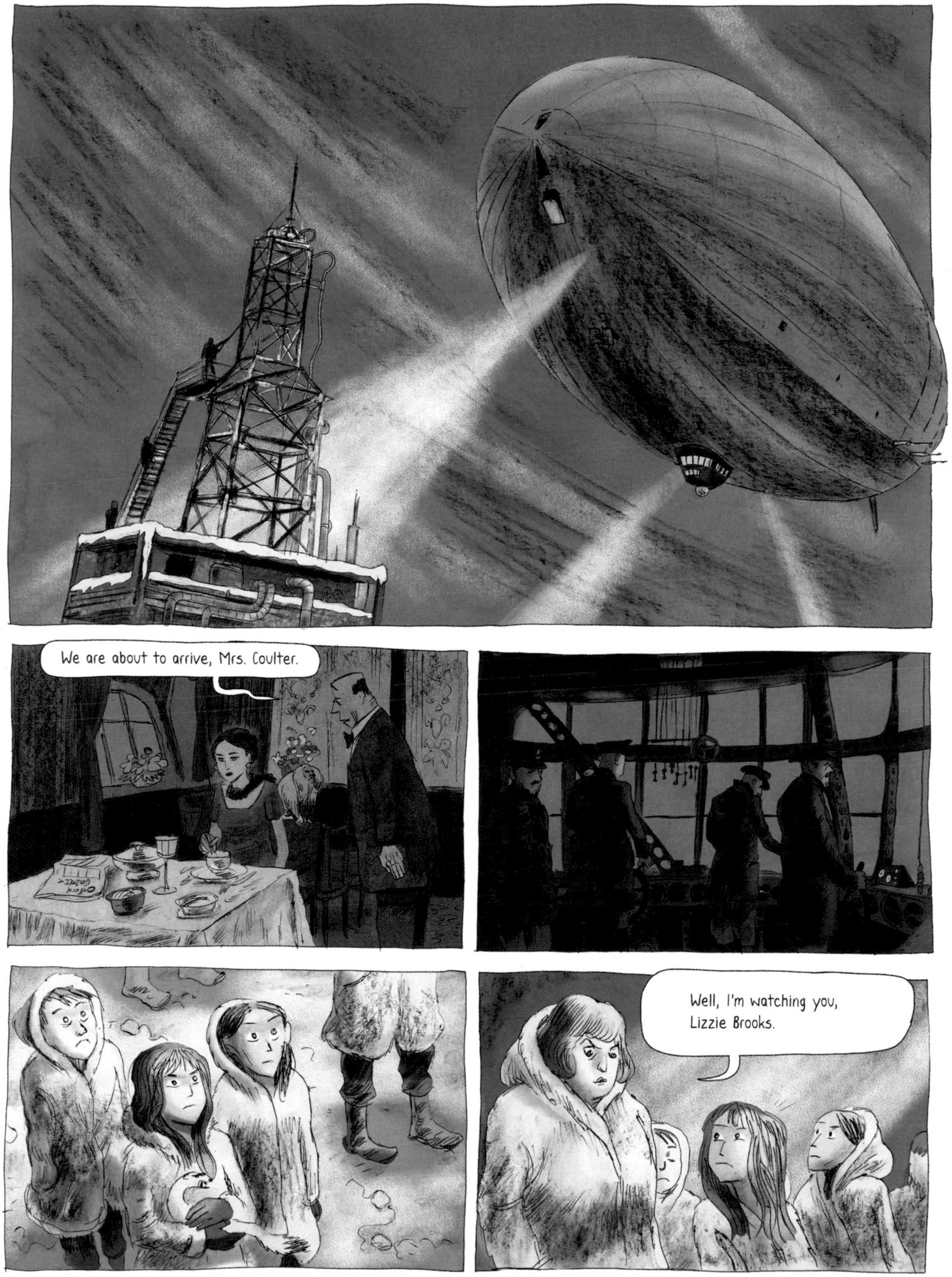
We are about to arrive, Mrs. Coulter.
Well, I'm watching you, Lizzie Brooks.

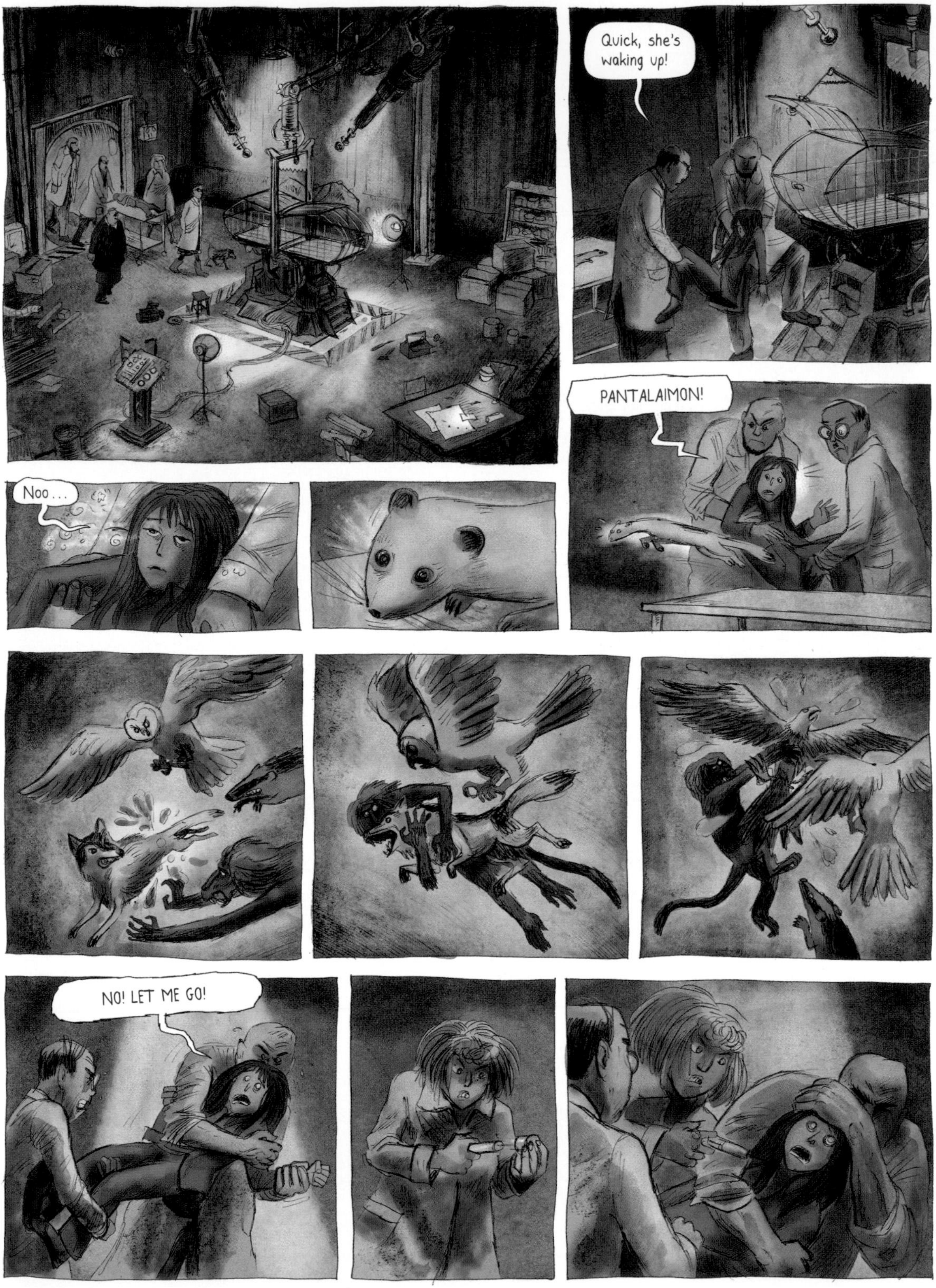
Quick, she's waking up!
PANTALAIMON!
Noo...
NO! LET ME GO!

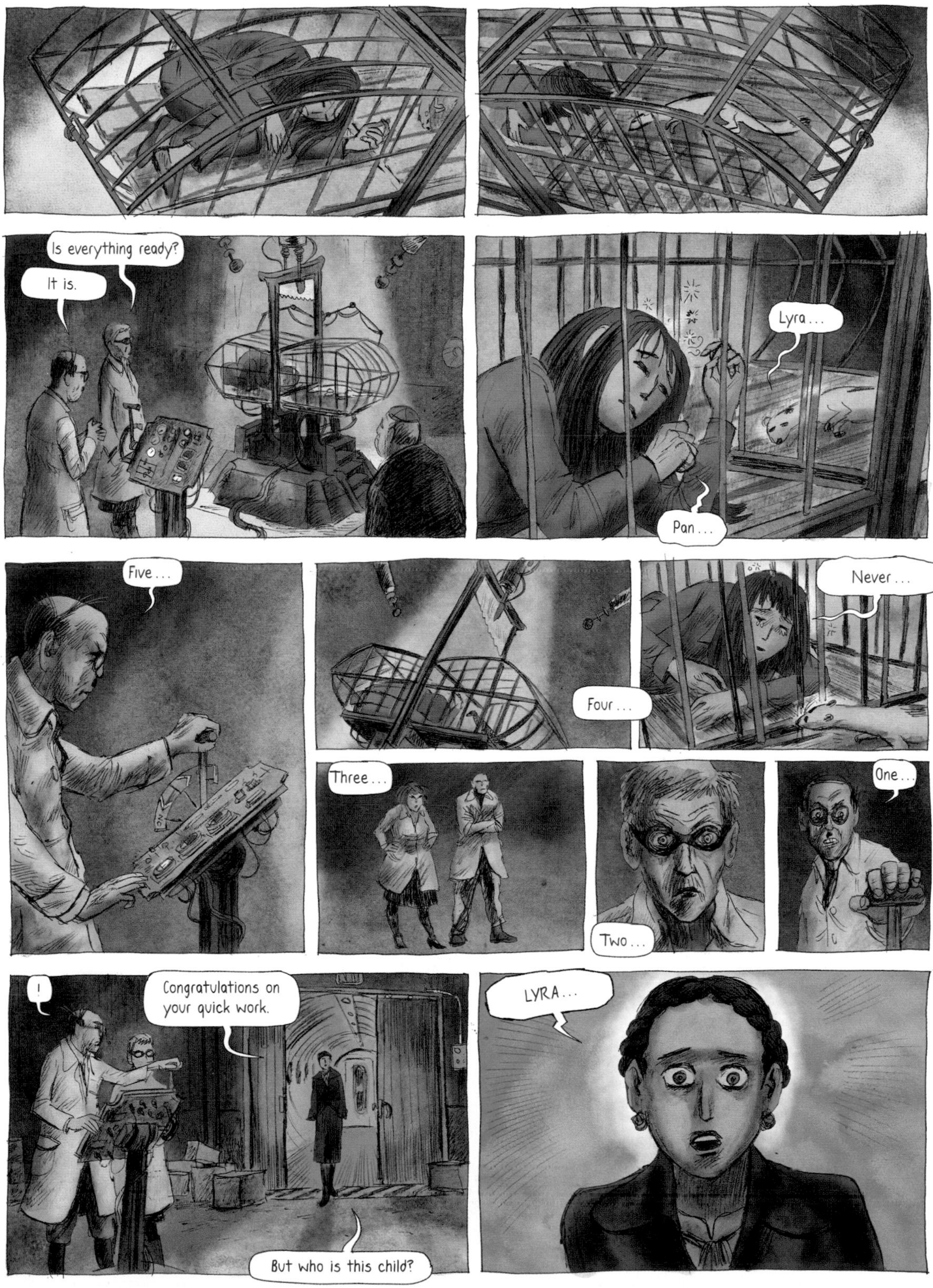
Is everything ready?
It is.
Lyra . . .
Pan . . .
Five . . .
Four . . .
Never . . .
Three . . .
Two . . .
One . . .
!
Congratulations on your quick work.
But who is this child?
LYRA . . .

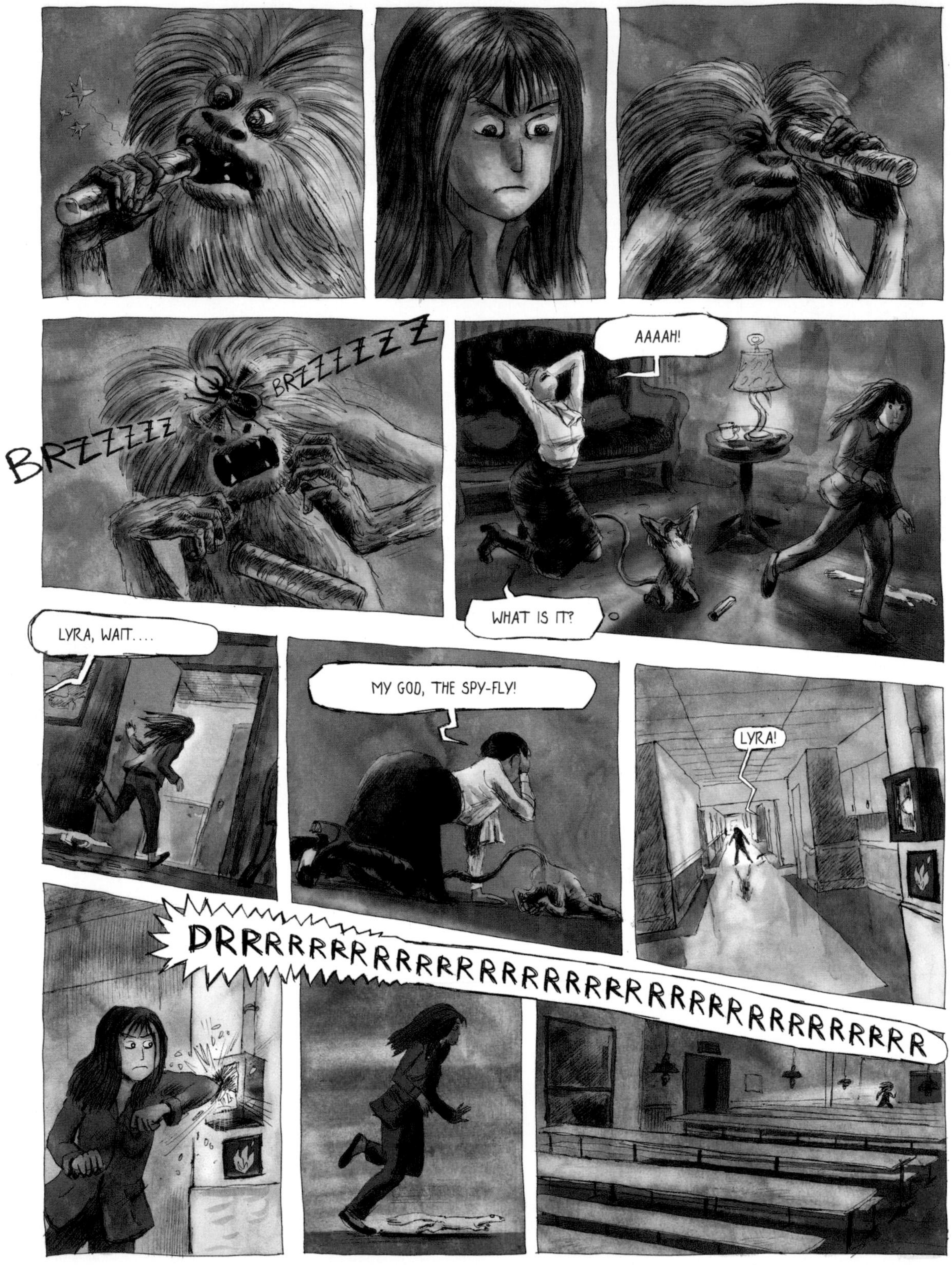
BRZZZZZZ
BRZZZZZZZZ
AAAAH!
WHAT IS IT?
LYRA, WAIT....
MY GOD, THE SPY-FLY!
LYRA!
DRRRRRRRRRRRRRRRRRRRRRRRRRRRRRRRRRRRRRRR

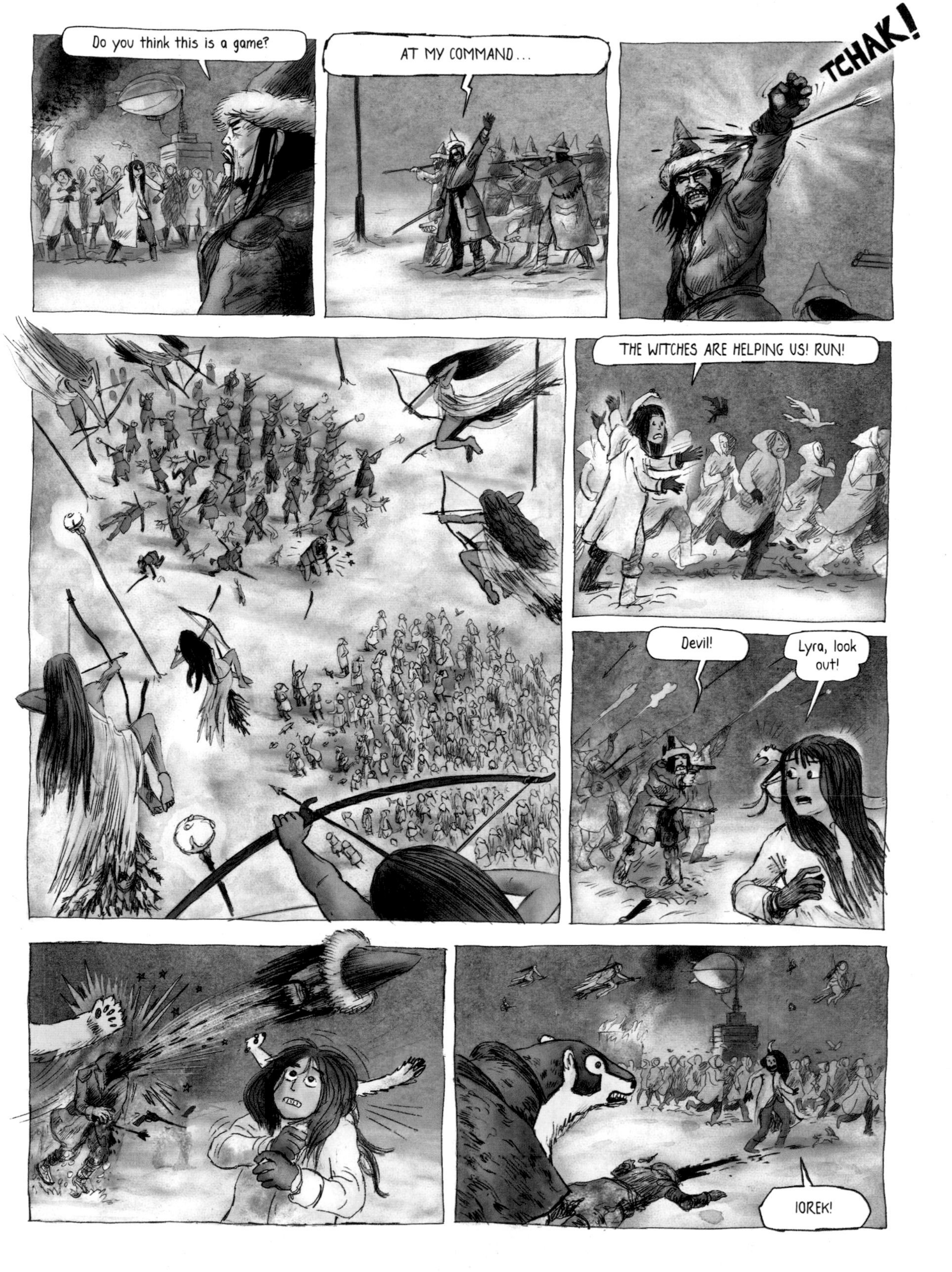

Do you think this is a game?
AT MY COMMAND...
TCHAK!
THE WITCHES ARE HELPING US! RUN!
Devil!
Lyra, look out!
IOREK!

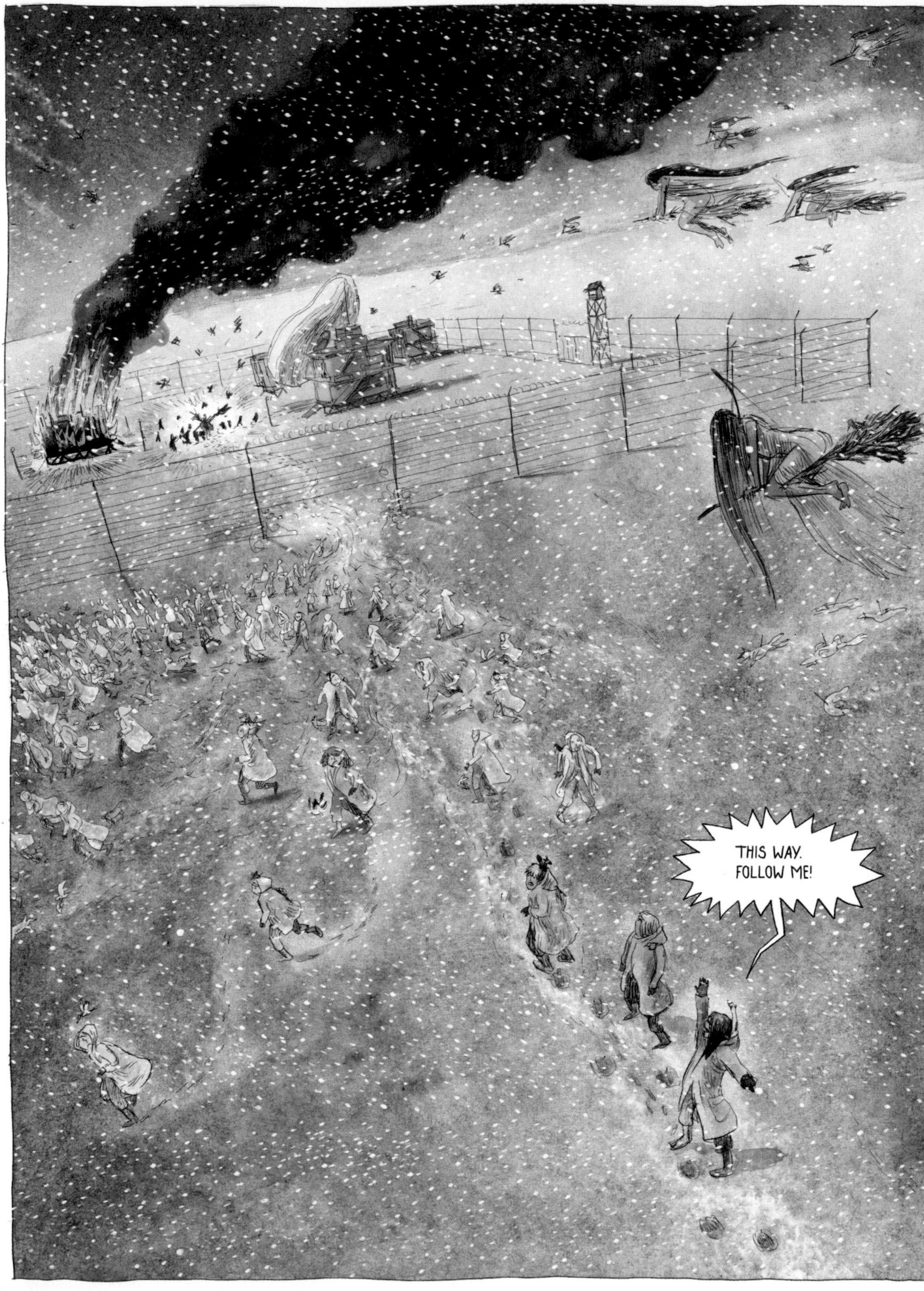
THIS WAY. FOLLOW ME!

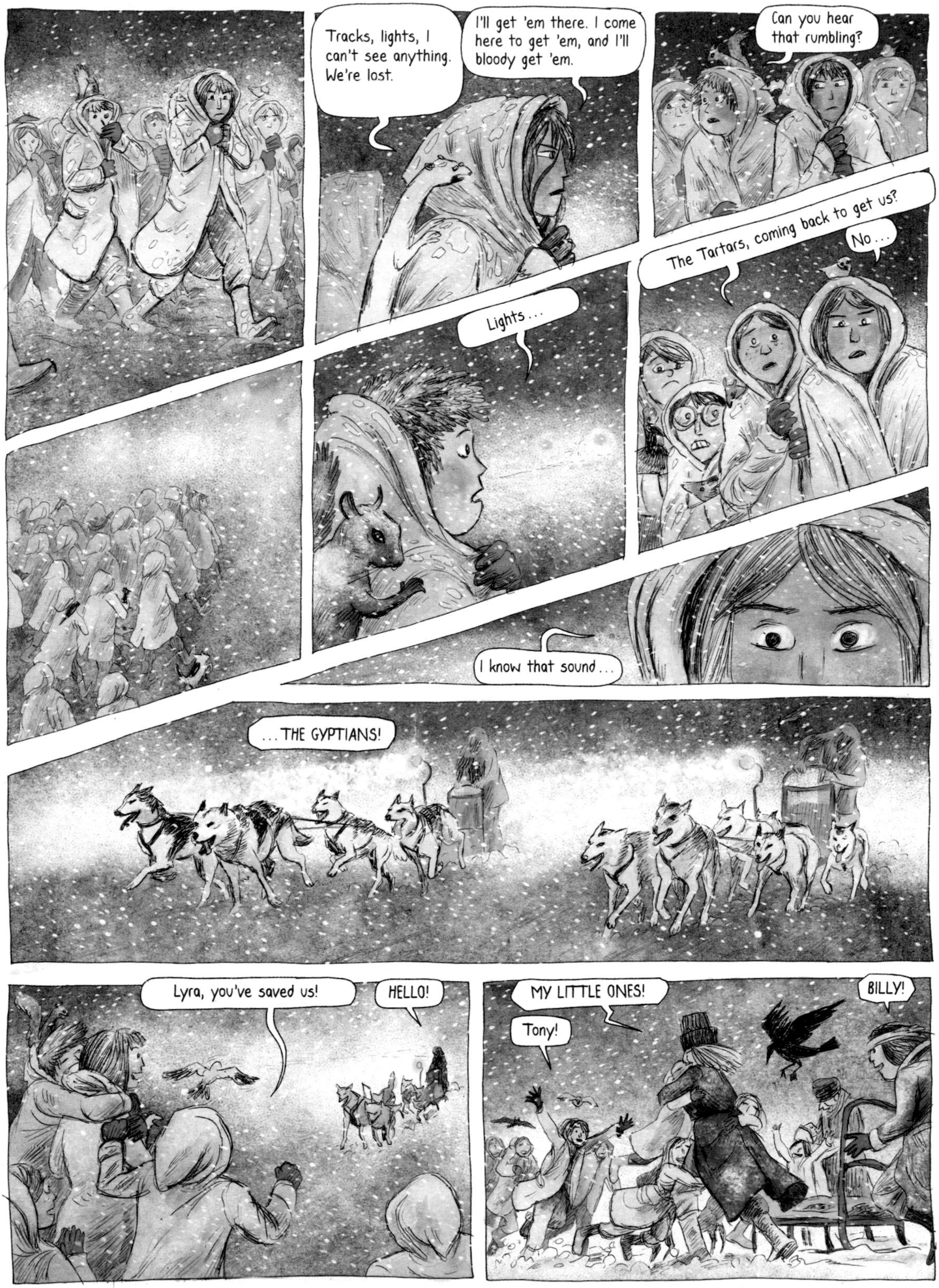
Tracks, lights, I can't see anything. We're lost.
I'll get 'em there. I come here to get 'em, and I'll bloody get 'em.
Can you hear that rumbling?
The Tartars, coming back to get us?
No . . .
Lights . . .
I know that sound . . .
. . . THE GYPTIANS!
Lyra, you've saved us!
HELLO!
MY LITTLE ONES!
Tony!
BILLY!

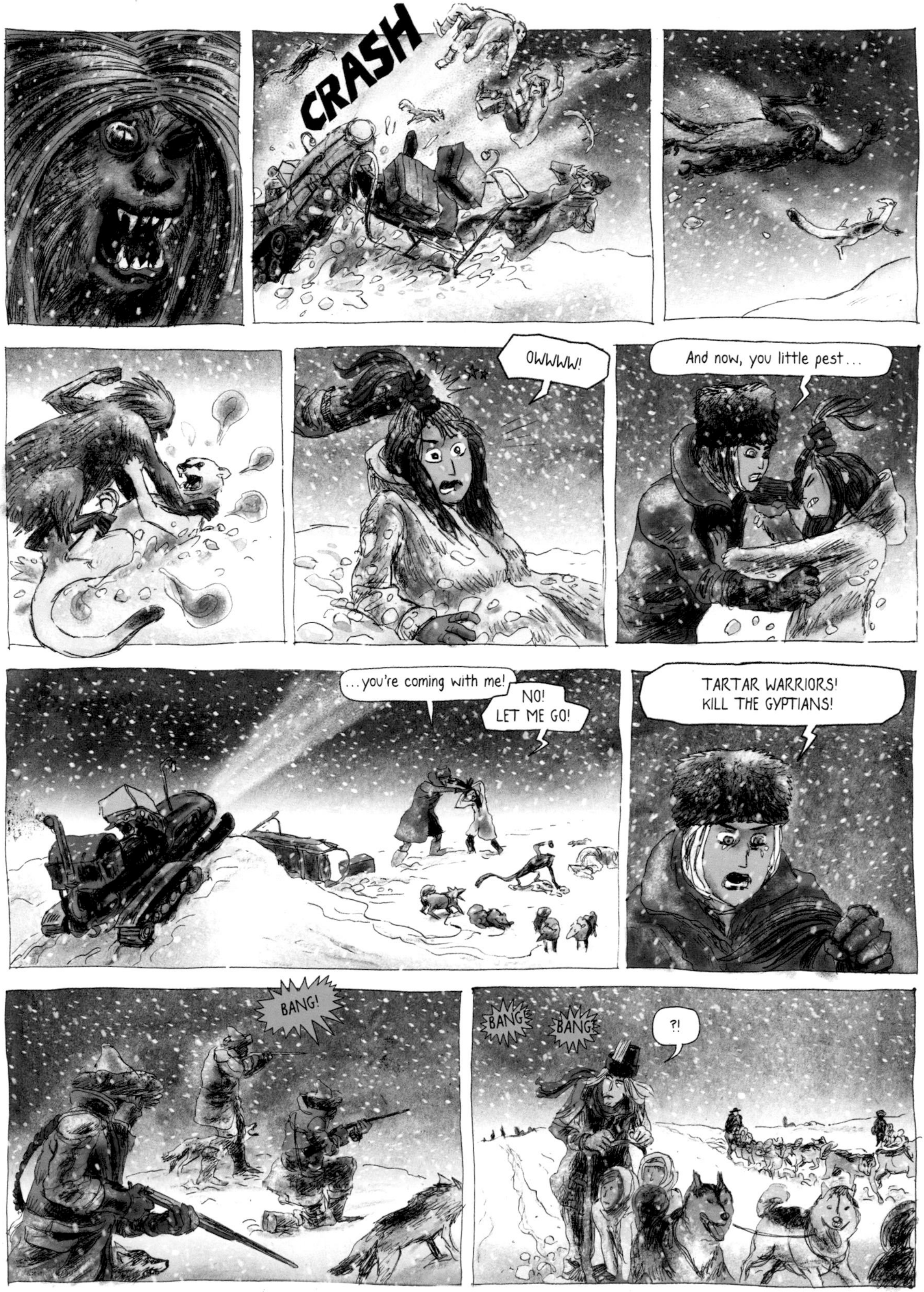
CRASH
OWWWW!
And now, you little pest...
...you're coming with me!
NO!
LET ME GO!
TARTAR WARRIORS!
KILL THE GYPTIANS!
BANG!
BANG
BANG
?!

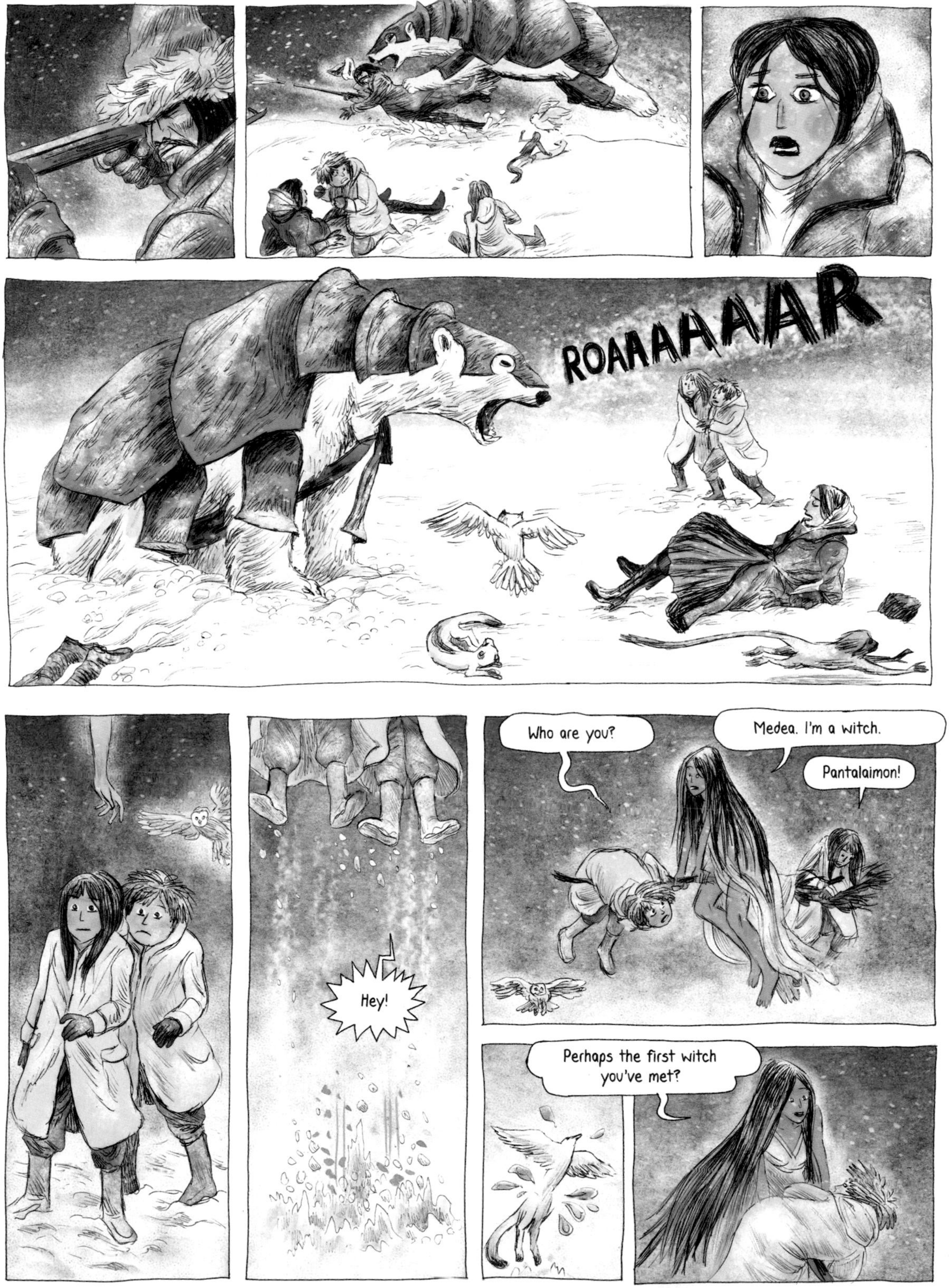
ROAAAAAAR
Hey!
Who are you?
Medea. I'm a witch.
Pantalaimon!
Perhaps the first witch you've met?

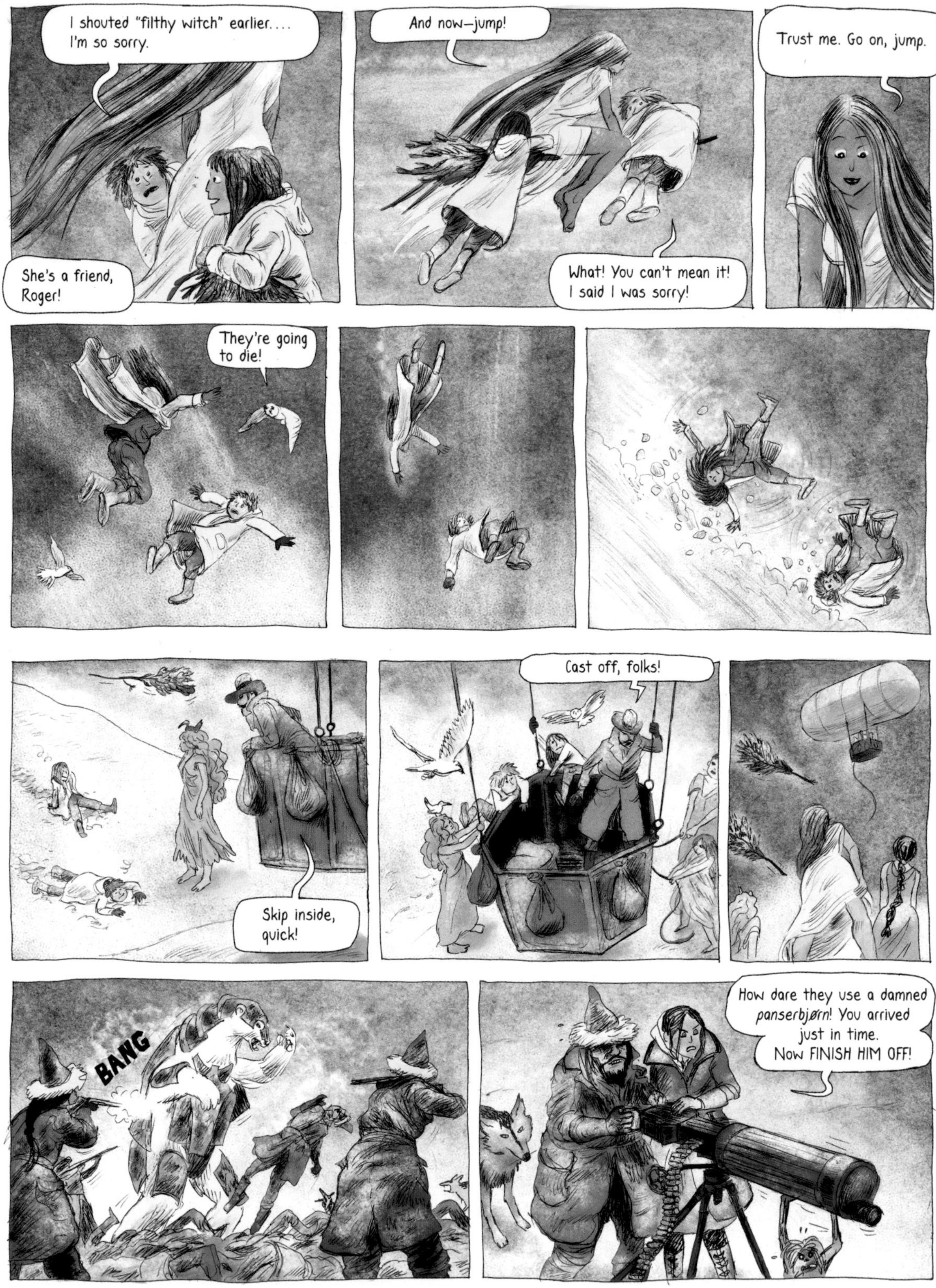
I shouted "filthy witch" earlier.... I'm so sorry.
She's a friend, Roger!
And now—jump!
What! You can't mean it! I said I was sorry!
Trust me. Go on, jump.
They're going to die!
Skip inside, quick!
Cast off, folks!
BANG
How dare they use a damned *panserbjørn*! You arrived just in time. Now FINISH HIM OFF!

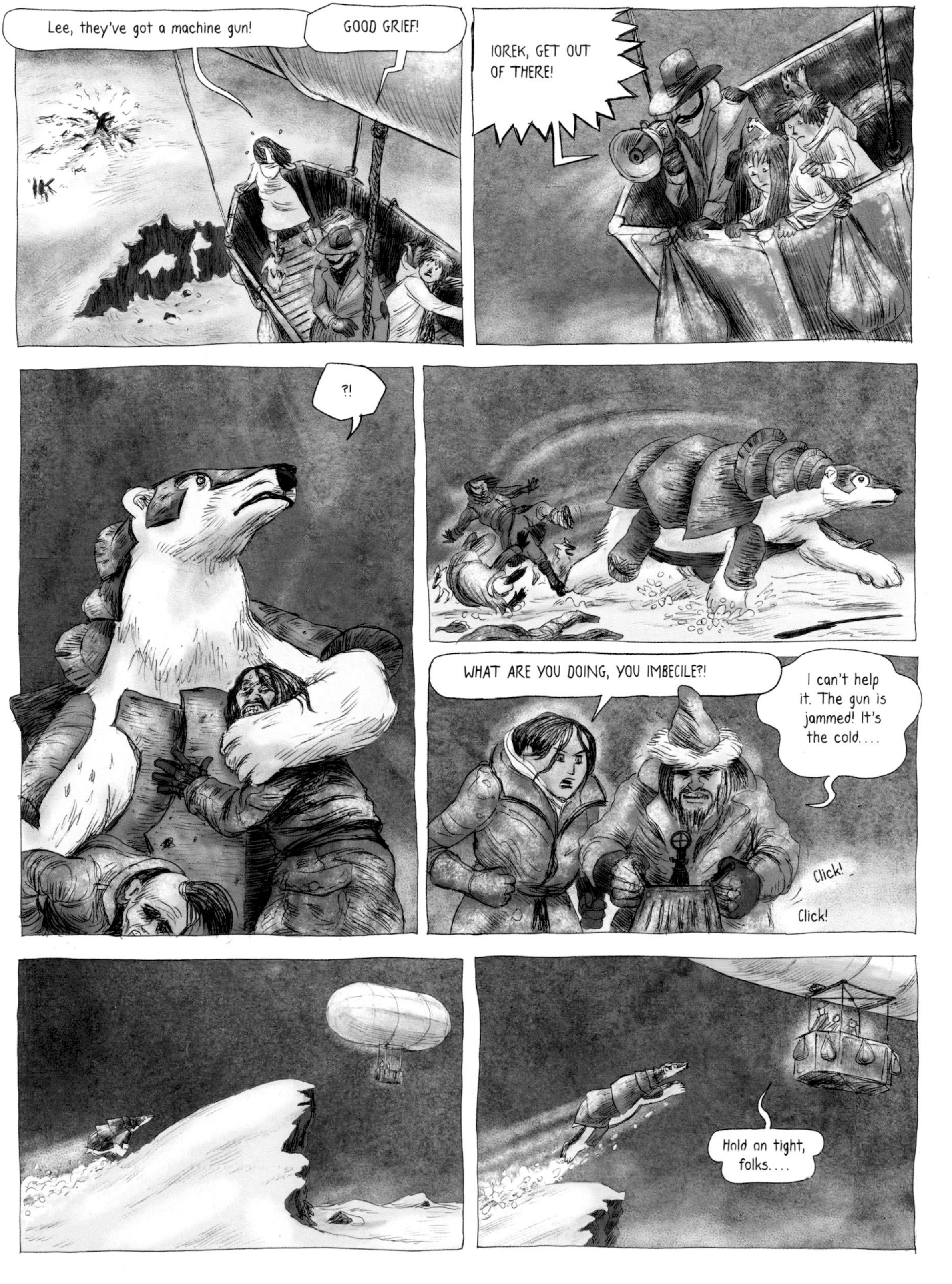
Lee, they've got a machine gun!
GOOD GRIEF!
IOREK, GET OUT OF THERE!
?!
WHAT ARE YOU DOING, YOU IMBECILE?!
I can't help it. The gun is jammed! It's the cold....
Click!
Click!
Hold on tight, folks....

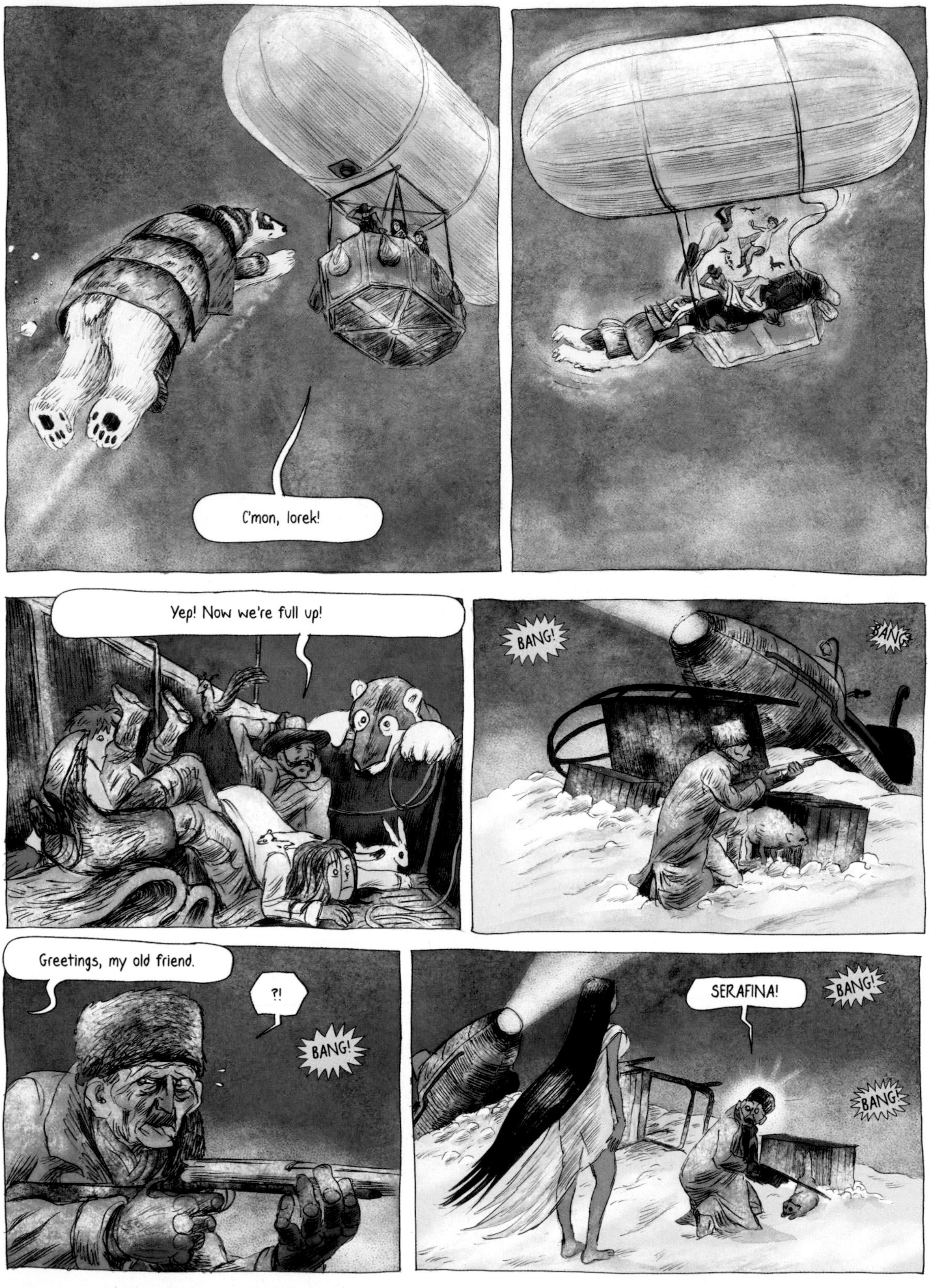

C'mon, Iorek!
Yep! Now we're full up!
BANG!
BANG!
Greetings, my old friend.
?!
BANG!
SERAFINA!
BANG!
BANG!

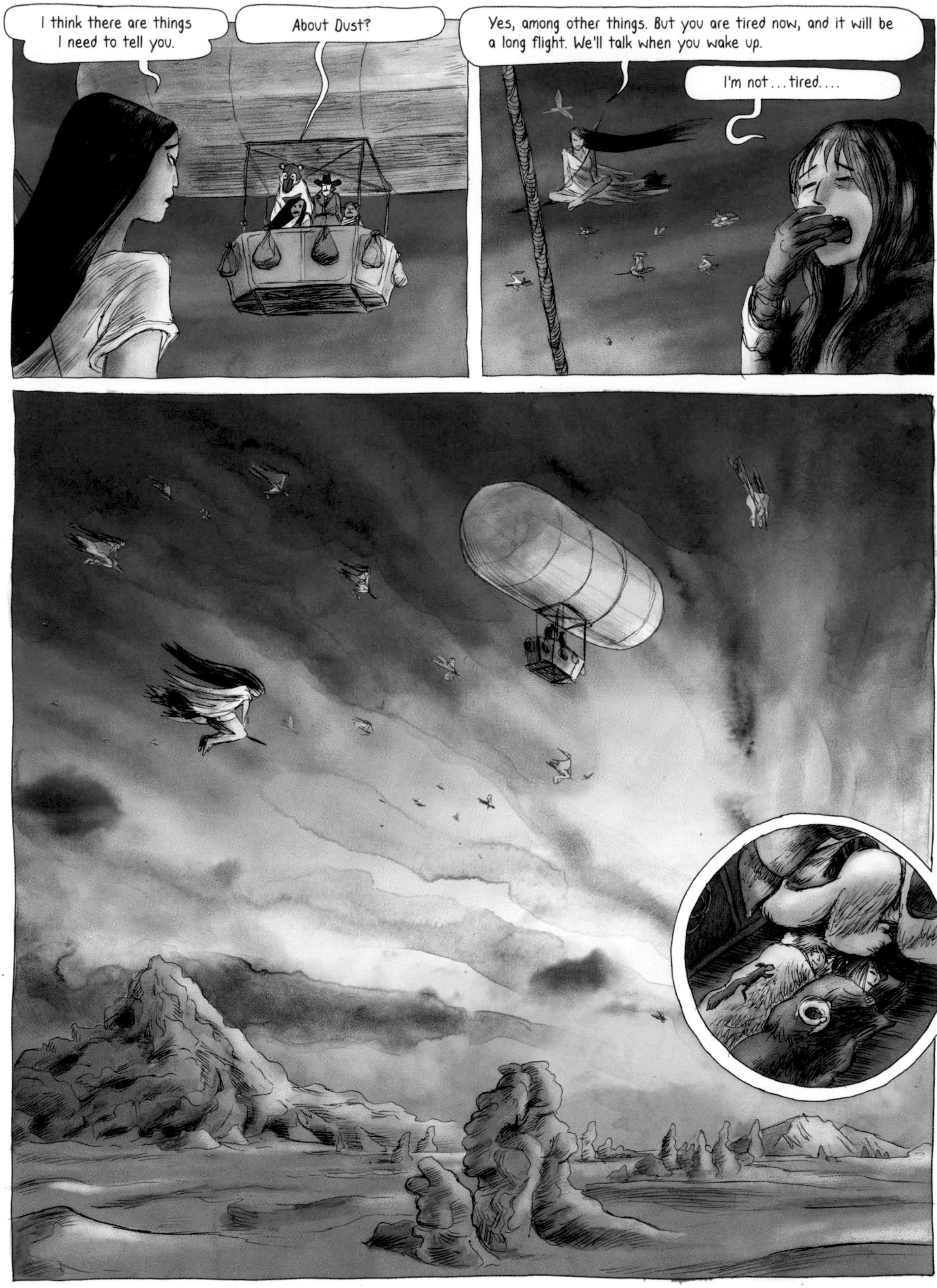

I think there are things I need to tell you.
About Dust?
Yes, among other things. But you are tired now, and it will be a long flight. We'll talk when you wake up.
I'm not... tired....

To be continued...

Lyra's journey will continue in

THE GOLDEN COMPASS
THE GRAPHIC NOVEL

VOLUME 3 coming in September 2017

HIS DARK MATERIALS

HIS DARK MATERIALS • BOOK I
INTERNATIONAL BESTSELLER
PHILIP PULLMAN
THE GOLDEN COMPASS

HIS DARK MATERIALS • BOOK II
PHILIP PULLMAN
THE SUBTLE KNIFE

HIS DARK MATERIALS • BOOK III
PHILIP PULLMAN
THE AMBER SPYGLASS

LYRA'S OXFORD
PHILIP PULLMAN

ONCE UPON A TIME IN THE NORTH
PHILIP PULLMAN

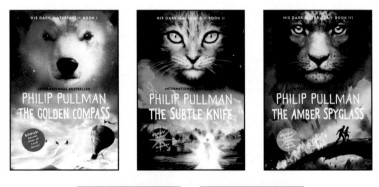

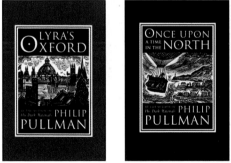

"Pullman's imagination soars. . . . A literary roller-coaster ride you won't want to miss." —*The Boston Globe*

"A literary masterpiece. . . . The most magnificent fantasy series since The Lord of the Rings." —*The Oregonian*

"Pullman is quite possibly a genius . . . using the lineaments of fantasy to tell the truth about the universal experience of growing up." —*Newsweek*